STEAM ROOM CONFIDENTIAL
Volume 5

JC Calciano

175 Publishing

Paperback ISBN: 979-8-9880054-8-3

Steam Room Confidential: Volume 5
by JC Calciano

For permissions and inquiries, contact
mail@cinema175.com.

Cover design by Miblart

Published in Los Angeles, California, U.S.A. by 175 Publishing, an imprint of Whitestone Acquisitions L.L.C.

Read more at JCCalciano.com

Table of Contents

Introduction

Cole faced a dilemma, unable to determine which was more scorching: the steam rooms he frequented or the captivating anecdotes shared by the guys within them.

During his latest visit to the steam room, he encountered a group of eight attractive men, each recounting a scandalous tale more alluring than the previous one. While some of these encounters blossomed into love, they all resulted in passionate liaisons that left a lasting impression.

Settling into the company of the group, Cole found a comfortable spot on the wooden bench. With a brief nod to his companions, he flexed his abs while loosening his towel, preparing to immerse himself in the ambiance.

Whether it was the warm, humid air or the presence of muscular men on either side of him sharing their most intimate experiences, the atmosphere grew increasingly intense. Remaining silent, Cole absorbed the stories told by his companions in the steamy mist, documenting each affair, each one more illicit than the next.

These are the stories he heard in the steam room that day.

Fearless Fireman

The alarm bell rang in the firehouse, signaling a blazing fire in downtown Kansas City. Wells was the first to gear up and jump behind the wheel of Engine 463. As the firehouse captain, he was adored by the community's citizens. No one in the company was stronger, smarter, or more compassionate than he was. Second in command to Wells was his best friend, Keith Tucker, who was musclebound, athletic, and handsome.

The two strapping men were the town's pride and its most eligible bachelors. Wells was the bigger of the two men and had a youthful appearance that gave him a high school star quarterback look rather than a rugged fireman. Keith was tall and striking in appearance, with bulging arms covered in tattoos. His weathered, handsome face donned a well-groomed, standard-issue fireman's mustache.

The two studly firefighters have been best friends for the last ten years. They instantly bonded when they met in high school, defending a nerdy first-year student from a sophomore bully. They have been inseparable ever since and have dedicated their lives to serving and protecting the members of their community.

Keith was a recent divorcee. Now single, he possessed sole custody of his daughter, Emily. At four feet tall, with long dark hair and a pixie face that was as sweet as it was innocent. Emily Tucker was the apple of her dad's eye and Well's beloved goddaughter. The trio was inseparable, forming their own little family unit.

Emily often referred to Wells as her "second father" because he frequently picked her up after school. Keith often felt a twinge of guilt, knowing that Wells had to spend time waiting outside the elementary school for Emily, but Wells was never bothered. In fact, he quite enjoyed it, particularly because it gave him the chance to steal glimpses of his secret crush, Emily's teacher, Mr. Saunders.

***

Mr. Saunders was blissfully unaware that amongst the sea of parents, a strapping fireman sat quietly in his truck and gazed hungrily upon his tight dress slacks and the form-fitting button-down shirt. Wells couldn't suppress a laugh at his own whimsical daydreams of having the scholarly hunk, Mr. Saunders, in his bed. Mr. Saunders was a stark contrast to the typical burly firefighter types Wells was accustomed to working with at the station. Instead, it was the nerdy, Clark Kent-esque, academic types that ignited Wells' passion, and Mr. Saunders fit that description perfectly.

***

As Emily emerged from her classroom, she instantly spotted Wells in his truck. Her face lit up at the sight of her *second* dad waiting patiently for her. She eagerly ran to him and jumped into his vehicle to be taken home. Wells warmly greeted her with a big kiss and snuggle. He began navigating the obstacle course of minivans filled with exhausted moms and sugar-infused children when he spotted Mr. Saunders walking over.

Wells's heart pounded at the sight of Mr. Saunders approaching. *Did I do something wrong? Am I allowed to pick up my goddaughter, or does it need to be a parent? Did Emily do anything wrong?* Wells panicked, thinking that something was amiss.

Mr. Saunders approached Wells' truck with a smile, his white teeth gleaming as he reached the passenger window. Despite a long day spent managing a room full of adolescents, his shirt and tie remained wrinkle-free, a testament to his meticulousness.

Wells thought, *be calm and collected. You're the fire brigade captain, not a teenage girl waiting for her high school crush to ask her to the prom!*

Mr. Saunders addressed Wells directly with his commanding, deep voice. Wells swooned as he imagined this stern yet compassionate teacher teaching him a lesson or two.

"Hello. My name's Jacob. The kids call me Mr. Saunders. I've noticed you picking up Emily when her dad was working. It's nice that she has someone as punctual and caring as you are looking after her. Would you give her father this invitation for me? It's for career day. I'm inviting students' parents to come into class and talk about their careers. I know Mr. Tucker is a fireman, and it would be nice if one of our local heroes would come in and educate the students about the occupation." Wells was so flummoxed by the butterflies in his stomach that he couldn't speak. Rather than giving him an articulate reply to the invitation. The words, "Gotcha. Will do. I'll give him the invite," stumbled out of his mouth.

Mr. Saunders nodded appreciatively and turned to walk back to his classroom. Wells caught himself staring at Mr. Saunders's impressively round, attractive glutes as he headed across the yard. He was grateful that Emily couldn't hear his thoughts as an entire litany of naughty fantasies ran through his head.

Wells snapped out of his dirty daydream when Emily proclaimed, "He's so nice, isn't he?" Wells replied immediately, "Yes, he certainly IS NICE."

Wells knew it was wrong to use Emily to do his recon, but he didn't know any other way to determine whether Mr. Saunders was coupled or not. As Emily gleefully sat waiting to be taken to her father, Wells opened a can of Red Bull energy drink and casually inquired, "Emily, do you know if there is a... Mrs. Saunders?" Emily instantly answered, "Mr. Saunders is a homo, just like you, Uncle Wells!"

Wells choked on his drink and spat it all over the interior of his truck. After regaining his composure, he continued somewhat sternly inquiring. "Emily, why would you call us that?"

Emily smiled innocently and explained, "Oh, Uncle, don't tell me you don't know that there are lots of different "sexuals." There are heterosexuals, homosexuals, bisexuals, transsexuals... and lots more. Would you like me to tell you about them all?"

Wells fought the urge to laugh as he instructed her, "You're right, Emily. I forgot about all the different "sexuals. But, in the future, you may not want to abbreviate those words when describing someone."

Emily was satisfied with that response and again reminded Wells to hurry so that she could get home to her dad.

***

Arriving at the firehouse was Emily's favorite part of her day. She was popular at the station, where the firefighters took turns spoiling her with hugs, treats, and gifts.

As Emily amused herself on the truck, Wells handed Keith the letter he had received earlier. "This is from Emily's teacher. He asked if you would talk to her classmates about your job. She told them you're a firefighter, and they want to meet you." Keith laughed, "Isn't this the dude you're hot for? It sounds like the perfect opportunity for you to get better acquainted with this guy. I'm sure Emily wouldn't mind if you took my place and spoke to the class." Wells instantly started making excuses. "No. I mean, yes, this is the teacher I like, but you're Emily's dad. He wants YOU to talk to the students. Not me!" Keith put a reassuring arm around Wells. "Dude, you seriously need to find a man. We all love you here, but you got to get yourself a boyfriend. This guy is perfect for you. I'll talk to Emily and see if she minds you standing in for me." Keith flashed Wells the same smile that broke a dozen young woman's hearts as he mischievously winked and teased, "You're Kansas City's second sexiest firefighter. What are you afraid of?"

Wells chuckled as he politely disagreed with his buddy about who should be first. "I'm THE sexiest firefighter. You're solidly in second place. I appreciate the confidence, but honestly, It's a bad idea. I'm not this guy's type." Keith decided he wasn't accepting any answer other than a "yes" from Wells. "Dude. You can't be afraid of rejection. You run into burning buildings. You don't flinch in the face of death. You're a badass. I have every confidence that you could muster the courage to ask some cute middle school teacher out on a date."

***

A week had passed, and career day was upon them. All the students were excited to have their friends and family come in to talk about their occupations. Emily was especially excited since she had a special request for Wells that day; she had asked him to please do his presentation in his firefighting uniform. Wells wasn't sure about showing up in his gear, but he was determined to make Emily happy and to give a good presentation, so he agreed to wear his uniform.

***

Three o'clock arrived, and his allotted time slot was almost upon him. Wells clunkily walked down the school's hall to room 316, where he was scheduled to appear. A quick knock on the door signaled to the teacher he had arrived and was ready to address the class. Mr. Saunders unlocked the door and opened it, finding Wells standing stoically in his caption's hat, boots, and yellow uniform.

Mr. Saunders gasped as he proclaimed, "Oh wow. Look at you!"

Wells instantly apologized, assuming it was too much and inappropriate to be wearing his regalia in the classroom.

Mr. Saunders fumbled over his words, clearly flustered. "No. No. This is wonderful. I know the students will enjoy experiencing the authenticity of having a real fireman in the classroom!" Wells felt better at Mr. Saunders's reassuring words and comforting smile. "Let's get you introduced. The kids are certainly in for a treat, as am I."

Wells was escorted to the front of the class and invited to make his presentation. Emily beamed with pride as Wells talked about her *second* father and the other men who worked passionately to protect the town's citizens and their homes. Students waved their hands, eager to ask questions of the giant, handsome hero in front of the room. Kelly McKee was the first to be picked and wondered, "Where do you live? Do you sleep at the firehouse?"

Wells smiled as he answered, "Most firemen live at home with their families. When an alarm goes off, they rush out of bed and into the station so that they may gear up and get on the truck to respond to the fire. I am the captain, so I have an apartment on the top floor of the firehouse. That's where I live."

The room erupted again as students begged, "pick me, pick me!" Ralphie Thomson was next with the question, "Do you really slide down a pole to get to the truck, or is that just in the movies?"

Wells' nerves had calmed down, and he began to enjoy answering the questions as he replied. "It's true. We have a brass pole that goes from the top floor down to the truck. It's the fastest way to get from the third floor to street level."

Mr. Saunders informed the students that the day was over and there was only time for one more question. Wells could see Emily's hand raised. It surprised him that she wanted to ask a question since she already knew so much about the profession. Wells couldn't pass up Emily, so he chose her to ask him her question. "I know you're all so brave and all, but is there anything you're afraid of?" Her inquiry stumped Wells. He stopped and thought for a minute before replying.

After a quick consideration, he confidently smiled and explained, "Yes. I get afraid. Fear protects us. It would be dangerous to be unafraid of scary things. The important thing is how you handle being afraid and the decisions you make when confronted with fear."

Mr. Saunders smiled at Well's answer. He was pleased with the intelligent and thoughtful response he gave the class. He then joined Wells in the front of the room. "Sorry, students, the day is over. Let's finish and thank everyone for their time. We must get ready to go home soon."

***

All the other students and parents had left when Mr. Saunders approached Wells to express his gratitude for his time. "You certainly were a hit today. I am grateful for your wisdom and expertise. I especially enjoyed your answer when Emily asked, "Is there anything you were afraid of?"

Wells bashfully looked down in an attempt to avoid eye contact. He knew the butterflies in his stomach would start fluttering if their eyes met again. Wells took a deep breath and replied, "Thank you for having me here today. It surprised me, too, when Emily asked if there was anything I was afraid of. I'm glad my answer seemed appropriate for the students, although it wasn't complete."

Mr. Saunders hesitantly inquired, "I'm sorry to ask you this, and maybe I shouldn't. But what is the complete answer to the question, "Is there anything you're afraid of?"

Wells took a deep breath, paused, looked Mr. Saunders directly in the face, and stated, "Frankly, I'm afraid that if I ask you on a date, you may say no." Wells exhaled with a mighty sigh, grateful to have gotten that burden off his chest.

Mr. Saunders blushed as he looked around the room for a rogue ear listening to them speak. He readied himself to answer, "Wells, I'm an educated man. Only a fool would say no to a date with you."

Wells nervously laughed, "Wonderful! How's Friday? I can make Dinner at the station. The guys tell me I'm quite the cook!"

Mr. Saunders found Wells' flustered response surprising and endearing. *How could this massive hunk of a man be so nervous around someone like me?* "I'll be looking forward to Friday night, then. I'm guessing I'll meet you at the firehouse?" he wondered.

Wells shot back, "Yes, that's where I live. The guys go home at seven, so the place will be all ours for the night. That is unless there's a fire that we need to attend to."

Emily started pulling on Wells' shirt, eager to leave and see her dad. Wells knew it was time to go, so he gave Mr. Saunders one last bashful glance before heading home.

***

Friday evening arrived. The firefighters took turns teasing Wells about his big date that night and how anxious he was about it all day.

Keith was quick to quiet the guys down. "Hey, give a guy a break. I remember when you all met your girlfriends and wives. You were just as nervous!" Keith wrapped his imposing arm around his buddy, pulling him in tightly as he squeezed and assured him, "Bro. You're an awesome guy. Be yourself, and he'll love you–if he doesn't, we know where his house is–he'll have Kansas city's entire fire brigade to answer to!"

Wells playfully freed himself from Keith's powerful grasp and thanked him for his sweet yet disturbing sentiment. Wells once again insisted all the men go home for the night so he could finish preparing for his date.

***

It was seven o'clock when a knock on the big oak doors of the firehouse signaled Mr. Saunders had arrived.

Wells thought, *Perfect timing! Hopefully, this goes well, and we won't be disturbed by an emergency tonight! Fingers crossed!*

Wells was on the top floor of his apartment when he heard the knock. He anxiously leaped for the pole in the center of the floor and quickly slid three stories down to the ground level where the truck was parked.

With a mighty heave, the large, heavy door creaked open, revealing Mr. Saunders dressed casually in a button-down shirt and blue chino slacks. He was holding a bottle of vintage wine and smiling innocently. He chuckled as he handed the bottle to Wells, saying, "I hope red pairs with the dinner you're preparing. It's supposed to be a terrific year." Wells' heart skipped at the sight of this shy, sweet, nerdy man. "Red's perfect. Thank you for bringing the bottle. I can't wait to open it. Dinner's almost ready, so if you'd like to follow me upstairs, we can eat, and then later, I can give you a tour of the station." Wells was amused at seeing his date, looking around wide-eyed with amazement at the station's large red trucks and equipment. He was clearly impressed with what he saw. Who wouldn't be? Firehouses are every man's fascination. Why should his date be any different?

***

Three flights up were an easy trek. Each of the men was in their late twenties and in excellent physical shape. When they reached Wells' apartment, Mr. Saunders noted how much he appreciated the tasteful décor and the aromatic smells coming from the kitchen.

"Wow. You weren't kidding when you said you were a good cook. It all smells fantastic."

Wells humbly responded, "The men always enjoy the meals I prepare for them. They work and train hard; the least I could do is to treat them to something delicious at the end of the day."

Now it was Mr. Saunders who had butterflies in his stomach. *How did I get so lucky?* He wondered. *A hulking, handsome firefighter who's thoughtful, kind, and can cook?*

Wells expertly opened the wine and set the table in preparation to eat. "Best to let the wine breathe. We want to get as much of the full-bodied flavor out of it as possible."

Mr. Saunders was grateful he was with a fireman at that moment since he was clearly overheating at the sight of Wells. He knew that if the fire he was experiencing himself wasn't extinguished soon, he'd burst into flames.

Wells was feeling his temperature rise, too–he was hot for teacher and had to do something about it quickly.

The two men stood silent, facing the other for what seemed to be a desperately long time without saying a word. Neither of them was sure who would make the first move. One thing was obvious; they were both smoldering and about to burst. Mr. Saunders made the first move as he slowly leaned forward, lips pursed, eyes closed, hungry to feel Wells' mouth pressed against his. The sudden blaring of the fire alarm caused Mr. Saunders to jump nearly out of his skin. The siren was short and ended quickly, but it was enough to scare the bejesus out of him. Short of breath, as his heart raced, he couldn't help but think.

What terrible luck; just as my fire started raging, another breaks out in town!

"I guess you will need to respond to that," Mr. Saunders stated with obvious disappointment. Wells laughed. "No. That's just one Alarm. Nothing urgent; my buddy Keith and the guys can handle it. I'm still yours for the night."

"You're mine for the night? I like the way that sounds!" Mr. Saunders replied with a glint in his eye. Wells was suddenly calm, cool, and collected. He knew that this date was going to go well, and he was right about Mr. Saunders; they were a perfect pairing, and he was about to ace this date with him. Wells playfully continued, "Yup. The only blaze I intend to respond to this evening is the one in my bed with you."

Mr. Saunders wasn't shy about what was being promised to him as he added, "Well, that's nice to hear. I'm guessing we'll have an eight-alarm fire tonight." Wells laughed as he explained, "Alarms only go up to five. Not eight." Mr. Saunders took

Well's hand and placed it firmly on the front of his pants.

Wells knew how to follow instructions, so he happily complied. Who was he to argue with a teacher? He was well aware of what he was being instructed to do. With a hearty squeeze, he realized the magnitude of Mr. Saunders's pun. *Indeed, he was correct. Eight it was!*

Wells quickly took him by the hand and escorted him into his bedroom as he explained, "Being a fireman, I'm an expert in getting out of my clothes quickly, but somehow, tonight, I just can't seem to do it fast enough." Mr. Saunders wholeheartedly agreed as the two men rapidly disrobed, eager to quench the fire burning within them as they tumbled into Wells' nearby bed. Their bodies were locked together in a fiery embrace. They knew the blaze they felt in their hearts wouldn't be extinguished quickly.

Vegas Bachelor Party

At thirty years old, Branden had convinced himself he would be single for the rest of his life. This wasn't due to a lack of suitors. His handsome, boyish looks and innocent demeanor made him stand out in a crowd. Branden wasn't interested in meeting other men at all since his heart already belonged to someone else–his best friend, Matt.

Matt was a rugged, gregarious extreme athlete who enjoyed outdoor activities like skydiving and white-water rafting. He loved pushing himself to the limit and spending time in nature. Branden was happy to join his friend on his crazy adventures, and as a result, the two men became fit, toned, and inseparable.

***

Branden and Matt met years earlier at the university, where they shared an interest in engineering. The two college buddies often spent hours locked away together in the evenings, preparing for class and working on their assignments. Often, as the friends huddled on the couch studying, their bodies would sometimes innocently touch. Matt's arm would casually rest on Branden's leg, or his leg would slightly rub against

Branden's foot. While Matt didn't give it a second thought when this happened, these interactions excited Branden in a way he dared not reveal to his friend. Branden's heart raced and his breathing became shallow if their flesh nonchalantly made a connection.

Matt knew Branden was probably gay, and he didn't care, his eyes and heart was elsewhere. He was too distracted by a sexy cross-fit instructor named Sheri to think about anything other than her. Sheri shared the same zest for life, sports, and extreme activities that he had, in addition to being beautiful and clever. Matt knew the moment he laid eyes on her in school that one day, she'd be his wife.

***

Years had passed, school was well behind them, and their friendship grew stronger. It was spring, and love was blossoming all around. Matt was excited to share some big news, so he invited his buddy for a beer at their favorite pub after work to talk. Branden already knew what his buddy was about to ask him, but he decided to fain ignorance and play along.

As the two men settled into their favorite booth, Matt beamed with an awkward, innocent grin, as he chuckled, "You know what I'm about to ask you, don't you?" Branden smiled, pretending to be surprised. "It's been quite a few years since I've been with Sheri, and it's time I popped the question."

While Branden was pleased for his friend's happiness, however, the words of him marrying anyone other than him stung like a billion bee stings to the heart. The man he loved was officially going to be someone else's. Nevertheless, he conjured a hearty laugh as he replied, "Dude, it's about time you made an honest woman out of her."

The two friends chuckled as Matt reached over and took his buddy's hand. Branden's heart pounded in his chest at the simple act of being touched by the man he secretly loved.

Matt spoke thoughtfully. "Branden, you're the most awesome guy I know, the brother I never had. It would be an honor if you'd be my best man at the wedding."

Branden became emotional. He tried to cover his tears of joy by loudly blurting out, "Dude, of course, I'll be your best bro at the wedding. Not even a question. Anything for you! What else do you need me to do?"

Matt laughed as he replied, "Nothing else. Just be a best man."

Branden casually corrected him, "You mean THE best man?"

"Yes," Matt chuckled as he continued, "Yes, THE best man, along with Sheri's friend Ashton." Matt knew he needed to clarify the confusion of his last statement. He continued, "Sheri asked me if her childhood friend Ashton could also be a best man at the wedding... is that cool with you? ...I told her you'd be chill with it. Do you mind if Sheri's bestie is also a "best man"?"

Branden took a long, deep breath. He was delighted for his friend and the news he had just shared, but the thought of a second-best man just seemed wrong.

Branden swallowed his pride and pretended to be happy as he answered, "Matt, we've been tight for over ten years. It's not about me. It's your day with your bride. If Sheri wants her friend to be a best man too, it's cool with me."

Matt gave his bro a big bear hug as he sincerely replied, "You're awesome. Really. I love you, man. Thanks for being so accommodating."

Branden melted inside as he soaked in the sensation of Matt's muscular arms hugging him. His embrace felt like a warm blanket, making him feel safe and happy. How could he ever say no to this man? Matt had his heart forever, and whether either of them ever admitted it, they both knew it.

"You'll like Ashton, I promise. I hung with him when I visited Sheri's parents' house in Denver. He's a cool guy. He'll be at the bachelor party. Trust me. You'll think he's great." Matt winked as he released his friend from their hug, signaling the waiter for another round of beers. Branden couldn't help but sarcastically reply, "I can't wait to meet him."

***

The bachelor party was upon them, and the guys drove to Vegas to go nuts for the next few days. Branden and Matt were the first to arrive at the hotel. Neither of them had been to Vegas before and had no idea what to expect. Matt noted how pleasantly surprised he was that the hotel was tasteful and sophisticated rather than garish and tacky as he had expected. An eager host greeted them with a pleasant "Welcome" and handed them two room keys. "Here you go, gentlemen. Everyone has been checked in. Please have a wonderful time. Thank you for staying with us and choosing our hotel. We received a note for the groom."

The host handed Matt a printed message from Ashton before turning to attend to the next guest checking in. "What's up? What does it say?" Branden asked.

Matt cleared his throat and read the memo: "It says, 'Good news, I'm now going to be able to come to the bachelor party after all! I'll be arriving late tonight, but I'll be there. Don't start the fun without me!'"

Matt was excited at the prospect of Ashton meeting Branden. He was convinced the two men would become fast friends. "Great, let's get Ashton another room." The host regretfully informed them that the hotel had been sold out for months and another room for their party would be impossible.

As Branden tried to devise a solution to the problem at hand, Matt offered his own answer. He wondered, "Would you be cool if I put Ashton in your room for the night? You've got double beds. There's only one king in my room. How do you feel about having a roommate this evening?" Branden had to suppress the urge to blurt out, "What the hell, Dude? I don't even know the guy!" But he knew it would be selfish to deny the groom his own room this weekend.

Branden swallowed his pride and put on an accommodating face. "Yeah, whatever is cool, man. I'm fine with Ashton crashing in my room tonight if that's what you want. We can get this all sorted out in the morning."

Matt quickly responded, "You're the best, man...best man...get it?" he chuckled at his joke, then continued to cheerfully suggest, "Let's get ready for the party. We can meet up with the rest of the guys at the bar at 7:00." With a hearty pat on the back and an excited twinkle in his eye, Matt turned and headed down the opposite hallway toward his own private room.

As Branden headed to the elevator, he couldn't help but feel like he disliked Ashton more and more.

***

Branden quickly stashed his bags in the room, changed into his gym gear, and crushed a serious workout in the hotel gym. He then returned to his room to iron his clothes to prepare for the evening.

Upon stepping into the bathroom to freshen up, he noted the impressive and spectacularly spacious shower. "This bathroom is the size of my apartment! I could just live in this room and have plenty of space to entertain." Branden mused to himself how luxurious the accommodations were as the hot water from the showerhead began spraying over his muscular, sweat-soaked physique. "I could get used to hanging in a place like this."

***

Post shower, it was time to hustle and get ready. His workout took longer than expected. He knew if he rushed, he'd barely be in time to meet up with the group. He quickly wrapped a small towel around his slender midsection and dashed towards where his clothes were laid out. As he unwrapped his towel from around his hips, standing naked in the middle of the room, a deep voice clearing his throat to signal his presence scared the life out of him.

<Cough Cough>

Branden yelped, "WHAT THE HELL? HOLY CRAP, DUDE!"

Instinctively, he covered himself with his hands, noting an intruder in his room. Branden fumbled to grab the towel off the floor and wrap it around himself again. A series of uncontrollable giggles emitted from the stranger in the room, who kept repeating,

"I am so sorry! I shouldn't be laughing. I'm such an asshole. I didn't mean to scare you."

Branden's anger quickly dissipated since the situation was so absurd. He knew the person standing there chuckling was likely Ashton, who innocently entered what he thought was his empty room. Try as he did; he couldn't be mad at a guy just walking into a hotel room he thought was not only his, but empty.

"I'm Ashton. I should have knocked. Seriously, my bad." Branden was now awkwardly covered up and joined in the laughter.

***

The sight of Ashton came as a shock to Branden. He didn't really think about what he would look like or the kind of guy he'd be. Ashton was a sharp-dressed, well-groomed, and articulate man in his twenties. A fine specimen of manhood indeed. Ordinarily, sun-kissed California boys weren't Branden's thing. Ashton's big green eyes, wavy blonde hair, and tanned, ripped body was oh-so-delicious. "I'm Branden," he stammered as a reply to Ashton's Hello. Branden attempted to look relaxed and casual despite the embarrassing fact that his towel suddenly had an unexpectedly large bulge in it.

Ashton reached out his hand, "Nice to meet you. Guess we're roomies for the weekend."

"Yeah, seems like it," Branden answered, attempting to cover up his undeniable state of arousal.

Ashton seemed oblivious to Branden's struggle as he continued his greeting by asking, "Matt said they didn't have enough rooms for everyone, so he bunked us up together. Is that alright?" Branden did his best to look suave and collected, although he was anything but. "Yeah, all good. It's fine sharing a room. No biggie. Let me get dressed now, and we'll go meet the rest of the guys." Branden scurried off behind the dresser, out of sight, to slip on his boxer briefs and tuck himself discretely behind the fly of his jeans.

***

Seven o'clock came and went. Fortunately, Branden was only fifteen minutes late to their designated meeting spot. The bar was bustling, and all the guys were dressed sharp yet casually. It was good to see all the guys together. Nothing was going to stand in the way of Matt having a good time tonight–Branden would make sure of it.

One of the guys signaled to the waitress to bring another round of tequila shots.

Another round? Already. Ah, it's going to be one of those nights!

Branden pretended to drink the shot by casually slipping the alcohol into his water glass. There was no way he would get sloppy drunk this early in the evening. Matt was eager to ask his friend, "Has Ashton arrived yet? What do you think?"

Branden simply replied. "Yeah, he's here. We met for a minute earlier. He'll be down in a bit to join us." Matt looked at his buddy earnestly as he requested, "Please give him a chance. Get to know him. I think you two will really hit it off."

Branden quietly thought, *I doubt it. Just because he's ridiculously hot doesn't mean this dude's gaining any favors with me.*

***

A second round of drinks arrived at the table, as did Ashton. The guys quickly introduced themselves and engaged in friendly conversation. The discussions soon devolved from work to sports to women. Pitchers of beer flowed, as did stories about the guy's "straight" adventures. Branden did his best to join in with the group, but as hard as he tried, he increasingly felt like the odd man out.

Ashton sat at the far end of the table with Matt's friends from work. He looked at home with these bros. Jokes and silly phrases quickly flew back and forth. Branden couldn't help but feel isolated and disheartened at how he didn't fit in with the group. Ashton frequently looked over to Branden with an empathetic gaze, sweet smile, or wink, but Branden wasn't interested in his attempts to be friends as he wondered,

What was this guy's game? Is he mocking me or just trying to make some kind of acknowledgment that he's Matt's new best friend and I'm on the way out?

Branden cut back on the few drinks he had since they were making him anxious and paranoid. No one seemed to notice or care that he wasn't drinking anymore. Beers and chaser shots came within minutes of each other. Everyone was getting smashed. Branden looked at his watch–the group had been drinking for three hours now, and the bachelor party was settling into the bar for the night.

"Hey guys, I got us all tickets to this fun 80's cover band concert. It starts in twenty minutes if you'd like to go. It's in this hotel, so we don't need to leave." Branden gave an excited smile and enthusiastic hand gesture to rally the troop, but no one at the table seemed to care about Branden's proposed activity. Ashton shouted in response, "That's awesome. Let's do it!" But he appeared to be alone in his enthusiasm for the show.

Matt quietly turned to Branden and pulled on his shirt collar. In a calculated deep, slow slur, he interjected, "Dude, that would be a blast. I'd do that... but I'm not exactly feeling so good."

Matt's face was flush, and his eyes glassy. He was seriously intoxicated. His erratic sway signaled he was in no shape to continue drinking this evening. "Hey guys, Matt's not looking so good. I'll bring him upstairs to his room and be right back." As if he was a pro at handling inebriated fraternity brothers, Branden swung Matt's arm over his head and onto his shoulder and helped him stand. The two men, now somewhat awkwardly, made their way toward the hotel's elevator.

***

Once inside the hotel room, Matt stumbled around, attempting to get undressed. As with most drunk guys, he had a serious case of the "I love you, mans." Branden tried to get him to drink water and lay down, but Matt insisted on telling him how much he appreciated and cherished him like a brother. Branden thought his sweet sentiments were cute and enjoyed the loving words he spoke, but still, the fact remained that Matt was intoxicated and needed to sleep off the booze he had consumed all night.

"Fine. I'll lay down. I'm tired anyway!" Matt asserted as he staggered across the room, trying to remove his shoes. "Careful, you'll fall. Let me do that," Branden insisted as he untied his laces for him. As Matt sat on his bed, he clumsily unbuttoned his shirt and struggled to peel it over his head as if he were a failed escape artist trapped in an impossible trick. With a mighty thump, Matt fell back onto the pillows of the bed, shirtless, wearing only his jeans and socks. Instinctively Branden unfastened his pants, unzipped his zipper, and removed his pants.

***

The room was dim, and the flickering neon light seeped in from the street, bathing Matt's pumped chest and chiseled abs in a warm red glow. It wasn't until Branden had Matt's pants around his ankles did he feel strange about disrobing his friend. Branden's sole intention was to make him comfortable so he could sleep through the night. But as Matt laid still, half-naked in his boxer briefs, looking ridiculously vulnerable and innocent, Branden wondered if he was wrong to find his friend as appealing as he did. He was instantly consumed with guilt at the prospect of having the thoughts he was having about his bestie.

Fight it as he did; the fantasy of reaching out and caressing Matt's gorgeous face consumed him. This is the man he loved and desired for the last ten years, now practically naked, lying within arm's reach. How could he not fantasize about cuddling up next to him and feeling his warm, muscular body pressed against his?

What the hell am I thinking? This is Matt. My best friend. I can't think about him like this. I can't be getting turned on by seeing my buddy like this!

Branden blamed it on the alcohol, but he knew he was sober. Even if he wasn't, it didn't excuse him from his wild fantasies about someone who was like a brother to him. Branden quickly covered Matt with a blanket, hurried out of the room, and returned to the party and the guys waiting for him at the bar.

***

Upon returning to the table, only Ashton remained. It seemed everyone from the group had already disbanded. Ashton explained, "all the guys went to some strip club. I figured I'd wait for you so you didn't return to an empty table. I'm up for going to the show you mentioned earlier if you'd like. I think an 80s concert sounds like a great idea."

Branden forced a smile, although he couldn't help but be peeved at the guys for leaving him. He replied in a defeated tone, "The show already started, so we'd be late anyway. If I'm honest, I'm kind of spent from traveling today, and I'd rather just head back to the room and chill."

Ashton hesitantly inquired, "I'm kind of feeling the same way. Do you mind if I join you, or do you want to be alone in the room for a while?" Branden was impressed at how thoughtful the question was. He also realized how considerate it was for him not to make him return to the bar alone. With a slight, warming smile, Branden replied, "It's your room too. If you're beat, feel free to join me."

***

Upon arriving in their room, Ashton reached into his suitcase and pulled out an expensive bottle of scotch. "Care for a nightcap?" Branden was all in for a drink before bed. At his point, he was now sober and felt like he needed a cocktail to take the edge off the day.

Ashton took two glasses from the bar and poured them drinks. "A toast to the happy couple as well as you and I meeting and hopefully becoming friends." Branden graciously took the glass from Ashton's hands and toasted back as they clinked their glasses. "To the happy couple."

It was now apparent to Ashton that Branden had little interest in getting to know him better or being friends. He was baffled at what he did to make this guy so indifferent to his attempt at friendship. After all, they were both the best friends of the bride and groom. Why not get along?

***

Ashton decided the best course of action with his roommate was just to go to sleep and try again tomorrow. "I'm going to crash if you don't mind. Feel free to watch TV if you want. The volume isn't going to bother me. I can sleep through anything." He proceeded to disrobe to change into his sleep attire. He unbuttoned his shirt, folded it, and placed it on the back of the side chair. Branden's inquisitive eyes peeked over at him, noticing his washboard abs and round ripe ass.

Bro's undoubtedly built. He probably got that ripped from surfing. With that ripped body and those impressively good looks, this guy checks all the boxes in the sexy department.

Branden tried desperately not to stare at his new roommate as he dropped his pants and kicked them into the corner.

Hmm. Tighty whites instead of boxers? DAMN! I'm not hating what I'm seeing right now.

Branden's heart raced at the seemingly unintentional show being provided by his roomie.

First, seeing his best friend, Matt, half naked on the bed, sprawled out in his underwear unconscious, and now this hot straight hunk sleeping in the same room as me. Why is the universe punishing me tonight?

Branden knew he needed some help getting through the evening, so he inquired, "I think I could use another drink if you don't mind. Can you pass me that bottle?" "Have as much as you'd like. The bottle's yours," Ashton answered without a thought.

Branden helped himself to another generous pour and situated himself in the chair in the far corner of the room. Ashton was now in his sweatpants. He was wearing them commando style with a sleeveless, form-fitting tee. Branden couldn't help but notice how clearly and distinctly he could see his roommate's state of arousal through the thin, worn fabric of his cotton pants. Branden couldn't help but think,

Any dude working with that size of equipment needs to start an OnlyFans page. I mean. WOW.

"You know, on second thought, maybe I'll join you for another drink," Ashton cleared his throat and gazed upon Branden with a distressed look. He continued, "Hey, not to be rude or weird about things, but I'm catching some serious frost coming my way from you. If I did something to piss you off, please let me know. I'd like to make this a fun weekend for everyone–Especially Matt. So, if you're mad at something I did, let me know, and I'll try to fix it." Branden didn't think that his disdain for Ashton was so obvious. He quickly replied, "No, Dude, I'm fine. You're good. I don't have a problem with you at all."

Ashton was confused.

Did he read Branden wrong? Maybe if they get to know each other better, he'll understand what's going on. Maybe he should try confiding in him.

Perhaps they're both going through the same emotions concerning this wedding.

"Well, if you're anything like me, you're struggling with this wedding." Branden was surprised at this statement, and his interest peaked as to what he was talking about. Upon clearing his throat and taking a long sip of scotch, he suspiciously inquired, "What do you have against this wedding? Do you not like Matt?

Ashton was quick to reply. "No. Matt's a great guy. He's perfect for Sheri, but…"

His eyes suddenly teared up as he choked out the following words, "I'll tell you a secret. I've just been kidding myself for all these years." Branden was on the edge of his seat, waiting for Ashton's big confession about his friend.

Finally, Ashton exclaimed, "I've been in love with Sheri for the last ten years. As much as I think your buddy Matt is a great guy and perfect for Sheri, I can't help but be a bit brokenhearted knowing that she will soon be someone else's bride.

Branden was stunned. He sat motionless. What do you say to something like that?

Is this bro in love with the girl my best friend is about to marry? No way!

Branden had to ask the obvious question. "So, if you're both so tight and love each other, why aren't you together then?"

Ashton's melancholy expression turned into a shy smile. "I could never marry someone I wasn't sexually attracted to."

Brendan was baffled as he simply stated, "Dude, she's smoking hot. She's every straight guy's fantasy! What's the problem?" Ashton's smile turned into an outright laugh as he wholeheartedly agreed. "Yes, you're right. She's every STRAIGHT GUY'S fantasy. Not mine. If only I were into women!"

Branden was stunned. He didn't know what to say. He was amazed that Ashton was gay and that no one had mentioned it to him before. *How did he not pick it up? Was his gaydar broken?*

Before Branden could reply or offer any comfort to him, Ashton continued, "I hope I'm not overstepping when I say this. Perhaps it's the two scotches talking, but I see how you look at Matt. You've got the same expression on your face when you're with him that I do with Sheri. It's the identical smile I have when she walks into the room. If I'm right, you've wished for as long as you've known him that he was gay, so you could be with him the way you want to be. Trust me, I know."

Branden was speechless. He knew that Ashton was right, and he just said out loud the words he dared not even think for the last decade. Ashton looked deeply into his eyes and waited for him to say something, but Branden couldn't find the words. Neither of them said a word. Instead of speaking, it was as if they knew what the other was thinking, what the other needed. The two men slowly leaned forward and softly pressed their lips against each other's lips.

Branden realized how long it's been since he'd been intimate with someone. He had waited so long for Matt to return his affection that he never physically or emotionally reached out to another man. Suddenly, with Ashton, he was excited in a way he had never been before. He felt comfortable, warm, and wonderful. What was this feeling? It was delightful and almost euphoric. Similar to a drug that had only good effects and nothing bad. His heart raced as his body tingled. He reached up and drew Ashton closer, kissing him more passionately than he'd ever kissed anyone.

The two men wanted the other out of their clothes desperately. Each reached over to the other and impatiently helped them strip from their wardrobes. Ashton hurriedly worked over Branden's dress shirt button by button, excited at the prospect of the tight, muscular torso that awaited him underneath.

Once shirtless, Branden's pants were next. Ashton cavalierly whipped his belt through the loops as he impatiently unfastened his jeans. Branden's breathing was shallow as he desperately desired to have Ashton in his bed. Between gasps, Branden confided, "I haven't been with many men. Please be patient if I'm not very good at this." Ashton chuckled as he nibbled on Branden's neck, replying, "Me, neither, but I can't help but think that whatever we're doing now–even if it's incorrect, is pretty damn fantastic." Branden knew where this was going and was all in for what would happen next.

Ashton then pulled his lips from Branden's mouth and, with a heavy gasp, suggested. "I'm not sure if you saw the bathroom we have yet, but it's pretty spectacular. What do you say we move this into the shower? I think you'll enjoy what I can do with a bar of soap." Branden appreciated the suggestion as he greedily pulled off Ashton's tee and slipped him out of his sweatpants. "A shower sounds perfect right now since all I'm having now are filthy thoughts." He teased as he followed Ashton's firm, naked, bubble butt into the next room.

***

The next day, all the bachelor party guys met up for brunch at the pool. Ashton asked Branden to apologize for his delay in joining them. A long table was set up next to a series of cabanas. Everyone had arrived early, and some were on their second mimosas by the time Branden showed up. Matt saved a special seat for him. Branden was pleased that Matt thought about holding him a place next to him.

Matt couldn't wait to apologize, "Sorry about getting so drunk last night that I passed out. I have no memory of even getting back to the room."

Branden simply stated, "no worries. After the group disbanded, I headed back upstairs myself." Matt was eager to hear Branden's thoughts about his roommate for the weekend. He cautiously broached the subject, "So, how did you do with Ashton sharing your room? I figured you two would either get along famously or kill each other. Since he's not here this morning, maybe I should grab my shovel and help dig a hole to help you dispose of the body."

Branden chuckled as he confided quietly, "He ended up being a good roommate. He's on his way down shortly. It turns out that Ashton's pretty cool, after all. I get why you like him so much, and you wanted him to be your other best man." Matt was confused as he put his mimosa down and asked, "Why would Ashton be MY best man? YOU'RE my best man. Ashton is going to be Sheri's BEST MAN." Matt could see that Branden was baffled by his statement. He clarified, "Sheri doesn't have a lot of female friends. She thought rather than asking a female she wasn't very friendly with to be her maid of honor; she'd rather have Ashton be her best man."

Branden was embarrassed for making such a silly mistake, even more so by being threatened by Ashton for replacing him in his friendship with Matt. Before Branden could explain himself, Matt confided, "Bud, you'll always be not only my best man but my best friend. No title or person could ever take away how I feel about you. You're my

Dude… forever. I love you man, and I always will." Branden's eyes teared up at the sweet words being spoken to him; however, knowing Matt as well as he did, his impish grin and mischievous smile revealed another story that needed to be told.

Branden playfully questioned the look on his friend's face. "I know that expression. What gives? What did you do that you need to confess?" Matt laughed, aware that his buddy had busted him. "Don't be mad, but I pretended that I couldn't get a room for Ashton at the hotel just so you two would have to bunk together and get to know each other better. I knew if you gave him a chance, you'd like him and become friends… hopefully more." Matt confessed with a wink and sly smile.

"Upset? I'm thrilled!" Branden exclaimed. "I had an amazing night last night, and I know Ashton did too! In fact, we decided not to go home with the rest of you tomorrow. We plan to spend a few more nights here… in the same room… in that amazing shower." Matt fist-bumped Branden as he boasted, "Go get 'em, Tiger. I knew you two would hit it off. I'm super psyched for both of you." Matt grinned as he went on to whisper, "You know they say, "What happens in Vegas, stays in Vegas."

Branden was quick to reply without hesitation. "Forget the "what happens in Vegas; stays in Vegas" Motto." I want the world to know that I met an awesome guy and had the best sex of my life here!"

Locker Room Romance

S oon-to-be sweet sixteen years old Gunner Sampson was already developing into a young man. His boyish, fresh face was giving way to the beginnings of facial hair, and the contours of a handsome teenager were starting to show. Gunner loved all sports and was remarkably good at them.

His favorite athletic pastime was football, and as a freshman at Seaport High School, he couldn't wait until he was eligible to try out for the team. Until then, he decided to sit on the bleachers and watch the team scrimmage. He believed that by studying the plays they ran and their practice routines, he might one day earn his way onto the team.

Gunner arrived at the football field like clockwork to watch the varsity team play. The lineup was impressive, and the players were all handsome, talented, and fit. Gunner wondered which of the athletes was the most attractive, but that question was instantly answered when Brad Barham jogged onto the field. Brad had a head of hair like no other player. It was wild and full, and his piercing blue eyes brilliantly complemented his tan, flawless skin.

***

One afternoon, just after scrimmaging, the team finished practicing and headed into the lockers. Gunner gathered his things to return home to study. It could have been his mind distracted with the images of how sexy Brad looked in his uniform that day or the adrenaline pumping through his youthful body, but as he grasped his phone, it fumbled from his fingers and tumbled down through the floorboards of the bleaches he sat on. Instinctively, like a chimpanzee on monkey bars, he squeezed himself behind the wooden boards and down underneath the steel structure to where his phone lay on the grass.

His cell was propped up against the brick wall of the auditorium, next to the large windows of the high school men's showers. As he approached the frosted glass, he noticed a small area on the window where the white privacy covering was scratched away, creating a dime-sized peephole. At first, Gunner didn't give his geography a second thought, but the laughing and merriment he could hear through the window made him curious about what was happening inside the locker room.

Gunner knew he shouldn't look through the hole, but the sound of horseplay inside the room made it impossible for him not to quickly glance at what was going on. Slowly, he pressed his cheek against the glass and focused his eye on what was happening inside.

Much to his surprise and delight was a pristine and perfect view of the football team showering. At first, Gunner fell back onto the grass. The shock and excitement were too much for him.

Wow! This is insane and so hot. What am I doing looking at the football team like this?

Gunner picked up his phone and decided it was best to depart quickly and never give this opportunity another thought. Try as he did to leave, he couldn't go without another quick peek.

Again, Gunner pressed his face against the glass and gazed into the room where the young athletes busied themselves washing. This time, in the shower closest to him, stood Brad Barham, the team's quarterback. The steaming water obstructed his view slightly, but not enough to hide the muscular, toned athlete with a perfect physique.

The young player was lathered up and unabashedly reveling in the hot water that cascaded down his sore, exhausted body. Gunner studied Brad intently. He wondered what it would feel like to run his hand over Brad's tight abs, well-defined pecs, and perfectly shaped ass.

The sight of this showering, wet stud excited Gunner in a way he hadn't felt before. Before he knew it, he found himself in a state of total arousal. His jeans now had an impressive bulge in them that suggested that he was not as young and innocent as his fresh face implied.

OMG. Now, look at what I've done. I'm totally turned on! I can't let anyone see me like this. I can't come out from under these bleachers until I calm down.

***

The next day, Gunner made sure to be there as the team once again practiced. He intently watched the team's plays and the coaches' strategies. Try as he did to focus on the sport, Gunner kept daydreaming about when the team would finish practice and head to the showers.

As soon as they are done with this scrimmage, I'm leaving. There is no way I will duck under the bleachers and peek in the window at Brad and the team showering again!

Wrong as he knew it was, Gunner couldn't help himself. He was fifteen years old, and his raging hormones got the best of him. As soon as the practice was over, he found himself eager to steal another quick peek in the locker room window. The team soon barreled into the showers, a dozen naked men anxious to rid themselves of the dirt that covered them and eager to treat their fatigued muscles to a blast of hot, soothing water.

Again, as if it was his shower head of choice, Brad arrived in the area nearest the window and began soaping himself up. He stood amongst the steam, slowly rubbing the hot water and shampoo into his dirt-smudged hair, then bent over to massage his sore, taught muscles. He seemed to be in no rush to leave the soothing shower anytime soon.

Oh, I've got to go! I can't handle this! If I see any more, I'm going to explode.

Gunner quickly pulled his eye away from the glass and attempted to calm his heart from beating out of his chest. He inhaled long and deliberately in an effort to stabilize his shallow breathing. He was determined to calm down before he headed home to the safety of his parent's house, far away from these torrid temptations that plagued him.

***

Weeks passed, and Gunner never missed attending a practice or a game. He also never missed a visit beneath the bleachers to enjoy a few minutes of Brad's showering routine. It was like clockwork that Brad was in the same shower stall, exactly at the precise time Gunner would arrive to enjoy the show his dream man unknowingly provided him.

***

School was soon over, and the senior class graduated. A prestigious college scouted Brad to play football for them with a full academic scholarship. So, with a golden opportunity ahead of him, he left the state to further his studies and career. Gunner was sad to see him go since the times he got to watch this studly hunk in the showers was the highlight of his year.

***

Now it was Gunner's turn to attend high school as a sophomore. He was the proper age to try out for the junior varsity football team, and he was excited to play a game he loved. Gunner was secretly scared at the prospect of showering in the location he had been spying on Brad for the last year. The thought of being in the same locker room where Brad and the team showered was both exciting and terrifying.

Luckily Brad is not going to be in the shower with me this season. If so, I'd surely be harder than a college-level algebra equation.

***

Gunner made the team during the very first tryouts. Fortunately, he was able to navigate changing in the locker room with the guys. He learned that if he arrived at the tail end of everyone's showers and got in and out quickly while keeping his mind focused on the sport, he'd be able to keep his libido in check and not get overly aroused around the guys.

***

Gunner fit in easily with the team and soon became its star player. Now at sixteen years old, his body developed rapidly. Vigorous cardio exercises, powerlifting, and good genetics helped him become powerful, imposing, and incredibly cut. He was admired by his teammates and respected by the coach. It was clear to all that even as a junior varsity player, he was destined for greatness in the game.

***

The following school year came and passed, as did the year after it. Before Gunner knew it, he was now eighteen and a Seaport High School senior. Gunner seemingly transitioned overnight. The awkward caterpillar who crawled under the bleachers to sneak a peek at the Varsity football team was now its star quarterback. He had indeed transformed into a beautiful butterfly, and everyone knew it.

As Gunner made his way to homeroom one morning. Coach Sullivan caught up with him in the hall. "Hey, son, wait up. Got a minute?" Gunner stopped and replied, "Sure, coach. Everything okay?" The slightly plump, older man warmly smiled and patted him on the back as he assured him. "Yeah. Great. I was just checking in with you. Are you going to be ready for the big game next week? Are you getting enough rest? Do you need me to talk to any of your teachers and tell them to go easy on the homework this week?"

Gunner laughed as he responded, "Thanks, coach. I appreciate you asking, but I'm good. I'm caught up with school and getting enough rest. I'll be in top form next week for the big game. Don't you worry about me!"

The coach sighed and mumbled as he began his exit. "I'm going to miss you, kid. If I only had a whole team of players like you. We'd be a pro team."

The coach shuffled down the hall and out of sight as Gunner reacted to the ringing bell, indicating he was now late for checking into class.

***

The following Friday arrived and it was now Homecoming weekend. The entire school showed up for the game that night. The bleachers were full of cheering students and parents alike. Everyone in the town was eager to see their beloved home team be victorious over their rival. The opening kick-off came, and the team executed every play with precision and enthusiasm. There was no question in anyone's mind that Gunner belonged on the field and deserved to be playing with the older students. The game seemed to be over before you could blink. The score was 14 to 21, and Seaport High School was victorious.

With thunderous applause from the stands, the team took a lap around the field as they waved to the fans, showing their appreciation for their support. The coach signaled it was time to hit the showers, get dressed, and then head to the bonfire to continue the homecoming celebration.

***

Gunner waited to hit the showers. It was mainly because he wanted to spend as little time with his incredibly hunky teammates in the showers as possible in fear that he'd become excited and embarrass himself.

Once the last of the players were finishing their showers, he stripped down, grabbed his toiletries, and began to rinse himself off from the mud in the field and the sweat that saturated his body from the adrenaline.

Ahhh, the hot water, the intense pressure, the clean, fresh soap. Perfection.

As Gunner relaxed and spread his arms open to capture as much of the delightful hot water as he could, he smiled, remembering Brad years earlier, who showered in the same stall after winning the big game, just like he was now. He didn't realize that the thought of Brad in the shower, looking as gorgeous as he was, excited him. Suddenly he looked down at himself.

Whoops. I guess. I'm getting turned on!

Gunner self-consciously looked around the lockers to see if anyone lingered behind.

Nope. I'm by myself. I'm alone. Luckily, no one could see me.

Gunner chuckled at himself as he innocently glanced over at the peephole he had peered through years earlier. He remembered how much pleasure it gave him to look at the sexy man who showered where he was now.

Much to Gunner's surprise, there was no light visible through the peephole. It wasn't transparent as it should be.

Could it be that there was someone on the other side looking in?

Upon closer inspection, Gunner could see an eyeball staring back at him. He jumped, startled by the leering eye, and instinctively covered himself with his hands.

What the heck? Someone found my spot and the hole in the window's tinting. I guess it's time to go!

Gunner quickly turned off the hot water and scampered out of the showers and behind a locker door so that he may get dressed in private and away from the peeping eye outside.

Who could be looking in? Was it another young man discovering his sexuality? Perhaps it was a girl looking for a glimpse at her favorite football player?

Whomever it was, Gunner was curious who was the lucky recipient of his steamy show in the shower was. He hurried to get dressed as he slipped on his jeans and shirt. Within minutes, he was clothed and rushed to exit the lockers in an attempt to find out who was looking into the men's locker room at him.

The school was empty. Homecoming activities had moved all the students, fans, and families to a nearby bonfire. Gunner rushed out the double doors to the auditorium where gym classes were held. He hadn't walked over fifty feet before a deep voice startled him. A light cough indicated that someone was in the room with him and wanted him to know it.

Could this be the peeping tom outside the window, or is someone else stalking me?

At first, Gunner didn't recognize the man standing in the shaded corner of the room, but upon closer inspection, his heart raced.

Is that Brad Barham? The star footballer who he was madly in lust for when he was a freshman?

Brad slowly approached him. With every step, he became more imposing. His muscular physique, broad shoulders, and chiseled face.

Holy smokes, he's even hotter than I remember!

Brad again cleared his throat. This time, it was to speak. The deep timbre of his voice sounded like the lead singer of a rock band.

"Nice game out there today. You're quite the player. I'm impressed."

Gunner began sweating. His heart pounded in his chest like a jackhammer. "Gee, thanks. That's quite a compliment coming from you."

Brad laughed. "So, you remember me? You know who I am?"

Gunner was quick to reply. "Of course, you graduated two years ago. You're Brad Barham. Probably the best quarterback this school had ever produced." Gunner paused before continuing. "You still playing ball?"

Brad smiled as he answered, "Thanks for that compliment, and yes, a pro league has scouted me. I can't say who yet, but it looks like I'll play for a great team next season."

Gunner's heart was settling into a steady, calm beat as his interest grew in this fantastic athlete's career.

"What brings you back to Seaport? Obviously, you watched today's game."

Brad made himself comfortable on the Bench as he man-spread his legs and leaned back against the wall. "I stopped in for Homecoming. I figured I'd check out the game.

Once everyone split, I figured I'd walk around the school and rekindle some old memories. I was curious to see if that old peephole in the window was still there. I figured I'd look to see what view it provided. Who knew the young man who watched me for a few years would take my place at my favorite showerhead, and now I'd be watching him wash up after a game?"

It shocked Gunner that it was Brad watching him in the locker just now. He was also amazed that all that time, he knew he was being watched and who it was who was spying on him. Without a thought,

Gunner defensively responded. "Well, I hope you enjoyed the show I just provided you with!"

Brad didn't miss a beat as he replied, "Actually, yes. I enjoyed it quite a bit. It was very, very hot!" Gunner was stunned since that wasn't the reply he expected to hear.

Brad continued with a confident tease, "Well, fairs fair. You watched me for the past year, so I watched you today. I also had the same reaction you did in the shower just now. I hope you were thinking of me when you got excited."

Gunner took a deep breath and carefully responded. "As a matter of fact. If you really must know, yes. I was thinking of you before."

Brad winked as he gave a sly grin. "I'm glad to hear it. I was hoping that impressive display was because of me." He paused as he spied out his surroundings and continued. "Well, since we both seem to be admirers of the other, and both are clearly still in an excited state. What do you say he return to the showers and see if we could do something about rinsing away these dirty thoughts we seem to be having?"

Before Brad could respond, Gunner unbuttoned his shirt with his left hand and grabbed the back of Brad's head with his right hand. He pulled him quickly towards him and pressed his lips to his. He had dreamt of this kiss for several long years and didn't want another second to pass before he got a piece of this smoldering stud he had fantasized about for years.

Brad eventually had to gasp for air as he caught his breath with a chuckle. "Wow. Quite the lip-lock for a sophomore. Impressive."

Gunner winked as he confidently replied, "You haven't seen anything yet. Come on, let's get you undressed. Your favorite showerhead is waiting for you; I mean us. I'll grab you a towel. You can share my bar of soap. I expect we'll work up quite a lather in the locker room today!"

Snow Bro

B
riggs hadn't been skiing in years. As a teenager, he loved the sport, but when he started studying for the state's bar exam in his mid-twenties, time slipped away. Sadly, other than his regular visits to the gym before work and his four-mile daily jogs, he didn't have the time to head up to the mountains and ski like he did when he was younger.

At thirty years old, Briggs was at the "top of his game" at work. He was tall, lean, and handsome, making his co-workers swoon with his sharply dressed attire. The way his striking face complimented a stylish suit made him look more like a model for a Brooks Brothers ad than an actual attorney.

One day, his boss Chad invited him to join him at his chalet for the weekend. The plan was for the two men to go over a big case that was up for review soon while partaking in a sport they both enjoyed.

"Come on, Briggs. You've worked here for six months now– join me. We'll ski, drink, and cruise guys. There's this hot instructor I eyeballed last time I was up there. I plan to pretend I'm a beginner and take a lesson from him. Guaranteed, I'll score this stud by Sunday night."

Briggs wasn't sure how it would be spending a whole weekend alone with Chad. He found his boss to be overly confident and brash at times. Chad was the quintessential hunky gym shark that seduced guys and never called them again. He embodied everything that Briggs disliked about the way dudes went about dating and seducing each other, but the fact remained Chad was his boss, and he didn't want to say "no" to one of the partners of the law firm he had just started working for.

"Sure. All work and no play make Briggs a dull boy, I guess," he joked as he accepted his boss's invitation. "I'd love to join you at your chateau to ski, but just as long as I can work a bit. These case notes must be completed by Wednesday."

Chad waved his hand as he dismissed Briggs, claiming, "I have every confidence you'll get it done. I hired you not only because you came highly recommended by your previous boss and are a smart lawyer, but also because you seemed like a cool guy and a team player. Let's just have a good time this weekend. The work will get done...eventually. Come to the office tomorrow ready to head out to the slopes after work. We'll jump in my Range Rover when five o'clock hits and drive up the mountain."

Briggs was looking forward to getting back to a sport he loved. That night, he had to dig through his old clothes and storage boxes which were packed with his gloves, scarves, and a coat. While reaching up to the top shelf of the closet where his goggles were boxed, he miscalculated the step down from the small ladder he used to access the top shelves. With a clumsy thump, he hit the floor hard. The sound of his body smacking against the wooden planks resembled a bag of wet cement being dropped from the roof. As Briggs lay on the floor feeling silly and clumsy, he knew that something was amiss with his ankle.

"Great. The day before we go skiing, I twist my leg. Perfect." Briggs continued to pack his things, hoping he'd be okay in the morning.

The next day, Briggs hobbled into the office carrying a sizeable overnight tote.

"Don't tell me you're bailing on me, Briggs," Chad called out from his office. "What's with the limping?"

"No, sir. I'm all packed. I'm sure I'll be able to ski. It's just a bit swollen today. I twisted it pretty badly last night, but I'm confident I'll be able to hit the moguls hard with you when we get to the mountain."

"That's the spirit. Push through your obstacles and never say die! Well, let's get a productive day in today, and we'll head up the hill as soon as I can get all these briefings off my desk."

Briggs did his best to stay off his ankle all day. He was convinced it was nothing to worry about, but still, rest would do it good, so he kept his foot elevated as much as possible throughout the day.

At about five o'clock, Chad called out in his booming voice, "Briggs, let's do this! Quitting time. Let's get out of here!" Briggs quickly packed his suitcase with his files and assorted paperwork he needed to complete by Monday and grabbed his gear. Time to head out for a weekend with the boss!

***

The ride up to the chateau was uneventful as both men sat quietly trudging up the snow-covered mountain road. Chad played his favorite podcast, "Story Time with Jack Turner," a collection of classic short stories masterfully told. Briggs was requested not to "talk shop" over the weekend. "Let's just ski, drink, and bro-out. This weekend should be about getting to know each other and shredding some serious slopes." In addition to planning on having a good time this weekend, Chad repeatedly bragged about how he intended to seduce the hot instructor he booked for two days' worth of private lessons.

Briggs was taken aback when they pulled up to the snow-covered Swiss-style mountain chateau Chad owned—first-class everything. Beautiful plush rugs, heavily wooded walls, and an imposing stone fireplace made this weekend's accommodations the perfect hideaway for two handsome studs.

"I had my caretaker build a fire and stock the bar and fridge. We'll be all set for the weekend regarding food and booze. All you've got to do tonight is unpack and join me for a drink by the fire."

"Done!" Briggs replied, excited to be in such a lush and grand space. He couldn't deny that a drink and a warm fire sounded great.

Chad almost instantly called through the cavernous cabin, "Don't dawdle in your room unpacking too long. I'm beat and going to crash early. This drink will knock me out, so get yourself settled and join me for a cocktail."

"I'll be right there. Pour me a glass of whatever you're having, and I'll join you in a minute," Briggs hollered back.

Next to the raging fire were two oversized leather chairs. A fur throw blanket thoughtfully slung across the arm of the chair made it almost comically cozy. Upon Briggs's arrival in the den, Chad quickly handed him a drink and invited him to unwind by the crackling blaze before them.

"Pretty damn nice, huh?" Chad asked, fully knowing the answer to the question. "These are the kind of perks that making partner in the firm affords you." He continued, "I'm only a few years older than you, and I'm making high-six figures. If you're as sharp as I think you are, you'll make partner even earlier than I did."

Briggs was flattered by Chad's compliment, although he wasn't sure if he was interested in the responsibilities of being a partner in a law firm. Sure, having lots of money is great, and luxuries like this are a treat, but Briggs wanted more from life than work and success. He desired companionship and valued time spent with family and loved ones. His interest lay more in finding the perfect man he could enjoy long vacations traveling the world with. Chad may be impressed with the material things, but Briggs valued the people in his life above any fancy home, car, or clothes.

***

That night Briggs slept like a log. Before he realized it, it was the following day.

Chad called up to Briggs' room at an ungodly early hour. "Coffee's up. Let's power a cup and get our skis. I've got my lesson with that hot stud instructor, and I don't want to be late."

Briggs rolled over in bed, groaning.

What I wouldn't give for just ten more minutes of sleep.

He knew asking Chad to chill out for a bit while he caught a few more "z's" wasn't going to happen. Instead, he shouted back, "Let me gear up. I'll be right down!" Briggs hopped out of bed, excited to ski, but the piercing pain in his ankle and the large inflammation around his foot told a different story about his plans for the afternoon.

Wow. That's worse than I thought. I'll never get a ski boot over that ankle! It looks like I'm stuck in the lodge today!

Briggs didn't want to dampen Chad's enthusiasm for skiing, so he dressed quickly and hobbled down the stairs.

As expected, standing near the front door, Chad was fully dressed with two to-go cups of coffee for them. "The lodge isn't very far. We can walk it." With a deep, cautious breath, Briggs broke the bad news to Chad about his sprain. "Chad, my ankle's swollen today, and it's seriously throbbing. I'll join you at the lodge now, but I won't be able to ski today." Chad didn't miss a beat. "That's okay. I've got my lessons. I wasn't going to ski with you anyway. If you're cool with working in the lodge, that's fine by me. Now, if you can walk to the lodge, let's get ourselves out the door. I don't want to be late for my lesson."

***

The lodge was nearby, and Briggs was able to walk there. A short trudge through the fresh powdered snow put them directly in front of the ski rental window. "I'll grab my skis and meet my instructor. Why don't you make yourself comfortable by the fire inside? When I take my lunch break, I'll join you," Chad told him.

Briggs was happy to comply. Even though he'd prefer skiing, getting caught up on all his work sounded like a better idea.

***

The inside of the lodge was toasty and inviting. It was constructed of heavy oak wood and decorated with heavy draperies. A large stone hearth with a roaring fire was the perfect place to set up shop for the day. A small table between the fireplace and a sizeable double-pane window was just the spot to make it the ideal location for today's office. Briggs could see the "SKI SCHOOL" entrance outside the large window. Beneath the sign stood a dashing, exuberant ski instructor. All Briggs could make out in the snow and glare was a gleaming smile, tight-fitting winter jacket, and ski pants that gave this young man a spectacular ass.

Well, I guess that's Chad's instructor. I'll give him one thing; he has excellent taste in men.

It was barely a moment later when Chad skied up to the young man, boosting a toothy smile and a flirty gaze. Briggs could tell that Chad was behaving like a schoolboy at a high school dance, nervously trying to gain favor with someone he had a crush on.

Briggs giggled at the silliness of the situation outside the window as he wrapped his hands around his hot coffee and settled into the paperwork to be sorted.

Time flew as Briggs trudged through the stack of legal documents before him. Before he realized how late it had become, a voice behind him startled him. "Getting a lot done? It's lunch. Care to join me for a sandwich and soup?" Food sounded great now, as did a break from work.

"I'd love it. I could use a rest. I'd love to hear about how your lesson is going."

Chad gave a bashful smile as he replied, "I think it's going well, but all the guy wants to do is teach me how to ski. He's not picking up on any of my subtle propositions. This dude may be straight after all." Chad said in a disappointed tone.

Briggs laughed. "Well, you probably should have found out if he was into guys before you booked two days' worth of ski lessons you didn't need with him."

Chad was quick to reply. "Hey, I'm not done yet. Even the straightest of guys get curious under the right conditions. I hope to provide those conditions later."

Briggs never understood the idea of trying to sleep with a straight man. He knew that some guys were into it. But not him. There were so many hot gay men. Why bother trying to convince a straight bro into experimenting?

Too much work. I'm too old to teach someone how to have gay sex. I want someone who's already good at it. Briggs chuckled to himself.

Lunch ended, and Chad announced, "Round two with my little "snow bro." Let's see how I do this afternoon!" Chad zipped up his coat, fastened his ski boots, and with a loud clunk, clunk clunk of his boots, made his way out of the lodge doors and back into the snow.

Briggs settled by the fire once again. He casually gazed out the window as Chad waved at him. Chad's instructor was now by his side. This time the sexy skier wasn't wearing goggles or a hat. Briggs could now clearly see why Chad was so taken with this man. His piercing eyes and unruly hair complemented a strong yet youthful handsome face. Nothing wrong with that stud.

Briggs laughed as his mind raced, and this opinion about sleeping with straight men was rethought.

I think I'm about to change my mind about straight boys now. I may actually put the work in to see if I could get that man into my bed.

As Briggs found himself getting lost in the hunky instructor's big, beautiful eyes, he was surprised when the instructor looked back at him and waved. BUSTED.

How could he even see me sitting in here? I guess I was looking a few seconds too long.

Briggs awkwardly waved back and then bashfully returned to his work, careful not to continue making eye contact with the handsome ski instructor.

Several hours again passed, and soon it was late afternoon. The familiar clunking of ski boots clattering on the boots approaching tipped Briggs off that Chad was finished for the day. "Well, still no answers. I invited him for a drink with me later, and he declined.

"What's up with that guy? I guess I'll have one more shot at him tomorrow—then I'll know if he's straight, gay, bi, or whatever." Chad chuckled to himself as he pondered the mystery of this hot instructor's sexuality.

Briggs gathered his things and packed his bags. "Your timing is perfect. I finished my work for the weekend. Now, it's time to relax and kick back. Let's do it then. I could use a drink," Chad loudly proclaimed as he headed for the lodge's front door.

The two men were no sooner at the Chalet before Chad took a flask out and started filling it with bourbon. "Nothing like a good twenty-year-old bourbon while hot tubbing to melt away the day's stress. Give me five minutes to slip into my trunks, and we'll head back to the lodge and hit the hot tub near the ski lift. It's a private jacuzzi that only a few people know about. There's never anyone in it. It's my favorite place on the mountain."

"Sounds like a plan to me," Briggs replied.

This weekend is turning out better than expected—time to kick back and unwind, he thought to himself as he put on his bathing suit and covered his legs with warm clothes for the trek to the hot tub.

Chad's phone rang just as they prepared to walk out the door. "Hold on, it's the office. Let me see what's up." Briggs feared this call wouldn't be a short conversation, and he was right. Chad's call droned on and on. It was apparent that a visit to the hot tub was becoming less and less of a reality. Chad decided he needed privacy for his call, so he quickly asked the caller to hold as he addressed Briggs. "Hey, this is going to take a while. Why don't you just head to the jacuzzi without me? I'll meet you there in a bit."

Briggs quickly nodded his head yes and gave a thumbs up. He didn't need to be told twice to enjoy a relaxing jacuzzi in the snow. With a quick zip of his jacket and a flask of bourbon in his pocket, he made his way through the snow to the hot tub behind the lodge.

The snow was piled high. White glimmering walls surrounded a large wooden tub. Tall pine trees created a picturesque backdrop for his quaint oasis. Briggs thought, It's curious how no one is here to enjoy this beautiful spot, I'd be in this tub every night if I lived around here.

As Briggs approached the steaming hot water of the jacuzzi, he could see someone already enjoying the hot tub.

I hope they don't mind a little company since this place is too damn inviting not to enjoy.

Briggs opened his coat and removed his jeans, revealing his swimsuit underneath. As he lowered himself into the steamy water, he recognized the other participant in the tub.

Could it be Chad's ski instructor? Be cool. Don't act like a silly teenager around a hot hunk.

"Hey. You look familiar," were the first words from the studly stranger's mouth. "Are you Chad's friend? The sexy lawyer who works for him who sprained his ankle and didn't ski today?"

"Hi. I'm Briggs. Yes, I'm Chad's friend. You must be the hot ski instructor he's taking lessons from?" Briggs decided to have a little fun with him.

Hey, fair's fair, he called me sexy; I'll return the favor and call him hot.

"I guess so," he bashfully answered." Chad spoke highly of you today during our lesson."

"Well, that's good to hear since he's my boss," Briggs replied with a smile. "I'm glad he likes my work."

The instructor realized he hadn't properly introduced himself yet as he reached out to shake Briggs's hand. "Hi, I'm Quinton."

"I'm Briggs. Nice to meet you," he quickly replied before continuing, "I'm sorry I couldn't ski today. I would have enjoyed taking a lesson with my friend Chad, but yes, I sprained my ankle the other day. It's not too bad, but I didn't think it was a good idea to ski on it either. It looks like I'll need to skip the slopes this weekend."

Quinton lifted himself out of the water, so his bare, defined chest was now visible. Briggs could tell he was a big man, most likely six feet three plus inches. His chest had the perfect smattering of chest hair, and the water cascading down between his cut six-pack abs made Briggs gasp at the sight of his flawless specimen of manhood.

"I really wish I could hang out and get to know you better, but unfortunately, I've got dinner plans in town in about a half-hour. I guess you'll be nursing your ankle in the lodge tomorrow as I instruct your buddy?"

Briggs caught his breath as his eyes fought to stay above the waistband of Quinton's wet, clingy swimsuit. "Ah. Yes. I guess I'll return to my usual spot in front of the fireplace tomorrow. If you get a chance, stop in and say hi. Perhaps you could join us for lunch? I know Chad would enjoy the company."

Quinton laughed as he simply replied, "Let me see what I can do. Nice meeting you today. I'll see you tomorrow."

Briggs quickly answered, "Yeah. I hope to see you tomorrow."

Quinton turned and stepped out of the hot tub. Briggs could feel himself get dizzy at the sight of this hunk's rock-hard glutes and muscular hairy legs. Quinton quickly wrapped a plush towel around himself, then disappeared with a wink and smile behind a mound of snow.

Briggs caught his breath and opened the flask of bourbon. He enjoyed a long, drawn sip as he sank lower in the hot tub and closed his eyes, savoring the view he had just enjoyed.

***

The next morning came quickly. Briggs slept like a log after his cocktails in the jacuzzi. The dry, crisp mountain air did wonders for his slumber. Like clockwork, Chad again called up from downstairs. "I'm heading to the mountain for my lesson. Care to walk over with me? If your ankle is better, you can take a lesson with me." Briggs stopped dead in his tracks. A lesson? Quinton in his tight ski pants and that killer smile? Dare I say yes? Briggs looked at his ankle. It looked better. The swelling went down, but could he fit his foot in a boot? Was a hot hunk worth further aggravating a sore tendon? Briggs laughed at his own silliness.

Why chance hurting myself more over a cute boy? What am I thinking?

He called down to Chad, "I'll walk over with you, but I'm afraid I'm still not able to join you to ski today."

Once at the lodge, Briggs sat in his favorite fireside chair next to the large window facing the slopes. He cozied himself to the crackling mantel and sipped his coffee while preparing his work for the day. Out the window, he could see Chad awaiting Quinton's arrival. He was blissfully ignorant that he and Briggs had met the evening prior.

Should I have mentioned I met his instructor in the hot tub last night? Would he be jealous?

As Briggs pondered whether there was any wrongdoing in his activities in the hot tub, he could see a different instructor greeting Chat outside. Chad looked into the lodge at Briggs and shrugged. Both Chad and Briggs wondered what had happened to Quinton today.

Why was another instructor skiing with him?

The answer to Briggs's question came soon enough when he looked up to see Quinton standing before him on crutches. "Oh my gosh! What happened? Are you okay?" Briggs quickly asked.

Quinton hobbled over and sat fireside. He had a sly grin on his face as he quietly answered.

"Nah. I'm fine–between you and me. I'm just pretending to have twisted my leg so I didn't have to work. I couldn't stand the thought of spending another day with your boss shamelessly flirting with me today. I thought it would be much more fun to take the day playing hooky and come in here so that I could shamelessly flirt with you instead."

Briggs laughed as he casually proclaimed, "Hey, they say all's fair in love and war." Quinton wholeheartedly agreed. The two men couldn't help but spend a long, smoldering moment staring into each other's eyes. They didn't speak, but volumes were said between them in the silence.

Finally, Quinton asked, "Hey, feel like jumping in the hot tub again? I feel cheated that we only spent a few minutes together last night."

Briggs hastily answered, "Now?!" Quinton replied instantly. "Yes, now. Why not?"

Briggs happily conceded, "Sure. Let's do it. I'll grab my swim trunks at the chateau and meet you there in 15 minutes."

Quinton had a better idea. "Well, actually, I'm staying in my uncle's house right around the corner. He's got an even nicer hot tub than the one behind the lodge that we could use. You're welcome to go change into your swim trunks if you'd like, but it seems like a waste of time since I'm only going to be taking them off you when we get in the water."

Briggs liked the sound of that but wondered what to say to Chad.

Quinton could see Briggs was deep in thought. "Wondering what your boss is going to think about us leaving together now?"

Briggs's voice slightly cracked as he meekly answered. "The thought did cross my mind."

Quinton leaned forward and kissed Briggs deeply, passionately. He leaned into his hungry mouth as Briggs closed his eyes and focused all senses on the smell, taste, and feelings of this stud's soft lips pressed on his. Briggs desperately didn't want this kiss to end. Both Briggs and Quinton chuckled as they could see Chad out the window with his mouth agape and a stunned expression on his face.

Quinton playfully chuckled, "Tell him that, unfortunately, he couldn't score the sexy ski instructor this weekend–but you did!"

Island Fever

The sun rose over the horizon, casting a golden glow on the serene waters surrounding a remote island. Dr. Evan Thompson, a marine biologist, stood at the edge of the Pacific Ocean, his eyes sparkling with excitement. His passion for the sea was palpable, and he couldn't wait to immerse himself in his research at this far-off location.

At 28 years old, Dr. Thompson had already been featured on the cover of several magazines. He took pride in his achievements in oceanographic studies. He also understood that the scientific journals showcased him as much for his striking good looks as for his scholarly contributions. Evan, as he preferred to be called, didn't frequent the gym, but his physique suggested otherwise. His muscular body was the result of swimming, snorkeling, and battling the resistance of salt water.

Despite his acclaim, Evan shunned the spotlight. Fame, wealth, and notoriety held little appeal for him. He was a reserved, shy individual who wished nothing more than to be alone with his research, seeking innovative ways to preserve the planet and its wildlife.

Indeed, he missed the companionship and warmth of another person, but most men he met left him disinterested. For this reason, he consistently conducted his studies in the most remote parts of the planet, embracing solitude.

***

Impatient to get started, Evan prepared to snorkel in the shallow tide pool just outside his door. He shed his travel-worn clothes and stood naked in the center of his laboratory. His hairless, lean muscular body could have been prepping for a spread in a hunky magazine.

"Should I bother with swim trunks? There's not another person for miles, possibly not even on the entire island. Why bother with clothes if they aren't needed?"

Evan chuckled, shyly reaching for his trunks. "I'm just too modest to swim au naturel quite yet. Maybe in time. For now, I'll stick to the appropriate snorkeling attire."

Evan was eager to explore the nearby reef around the bend, hidden off the most secluded part of Starfish Island. This island was a small tropical paradise, absent from any map or Google Earth search. It was a tiny, pristine ecosystem known only to a select few marine biologists fortunate enough to be in on the secret. The adjacent cove was a hidden treasure, teeming with life.

Evan marveled at the vibrant diversity of marine creatures that called this place home - from colorful fish darting through the crystal-clear waters to tiny crabs scurrying along the sandy floor. He was thrilled to be conducting a study on the impact of climate change on these fragile ecosystems and was determined to find ways to protect them.

***

Evan splashed through the crystal-clear water as he strolled down the beach. The warm yet refreshing water lapped at his ankles. He couldn't help but smile as he watched marine life darting between his legs.

As he ventured deeper toward the tidal pool, he spotted something unusual floating in the reef. His heart quickened; something was amiss. Whatever it was, it clearly didn't belong there. As Evan drew closer, his breath quickened. Could it be? Yes, it was a person! Perhaps a shipwrecked sailor from a vessel gone astray? Whoever it was, the man was unconscious and evidently in distress. Evan hastily abandoned his snorkeling gear and rushed to the aid of the stricken individual.

As he neared the shallow pool of water, his eyes deceived him. What was he seeing? A handsome, muscular man entangled with a giant sea creature? Was he about to encounter a gruesome reminder that humans may not be as superior on the food chain as they believe? As Evan closed in, the scene grew even more bizarre. Now, less than ten feet away, he beheld what seemed to be a mythical creature straight from folklore and his dreams - a merman!

What was happening? Was this some elaborate prank? It couldn't possibly be real!

Regardless of his disbelief, one thing was clear; the being was in trouble.

Evan quickly knelt beside the half-man, half-sea creature. The being's upper body was stunningly fit; each muscle was clearly defined, his arms and pectorals rippling with strength. The tail, a brilliant kaleidoscope of iridescent hues, glistened in the serene water, half-submerged. The creature's masculine face outshone any handsome man Evan had ever encountered. His complexion was smooth and flawless; his hair, a lush, long mane the color of dark amber and sand, framed a solid, pronounced jawline.

Just being near this majestic creature was overwhelming. Evan quickly checked for a pulse on its neck. It was faint. He employed his biological expertise to try to revive the beast. Given the human-like upper body of the merman, CPR seemed like a plausible treatment option. Evan tilted the merman's head back and blew forcefully into his mouth, rhythmically compressing his chest. After several tense minutes, the merman coughed loudly.

Water sprayed from his mouth as his lungs refilled with air. Evan recoiled, unsure whether he was more frightened or surprised that administering air to an aquatic creature was the right approach. He was astounded that providing oxygen could potentially save its life.

The creature was weak and disoriented. Evan knew he had to rescue him from the reef, so he swiftly set up a makeshift tank in his nearby laboratory, intending to transport and house the creature there as he attempted to nurse it back to health.

***

Each day, Evan attended to the creature's wounds and bruises. He found himself increasingly captivated by the merman's extraordinary beauty and majesty. Even though the merman remained unconscious, his healing process was remarkably swift. With each passing day, there was a notable improvement in his color and strength.

Less than two days later, the creature awoke from his unresponsive state. Evan was sitting at his desk, not ten feet from the aquarium that housed his recuperating guest, when a deep voice addressed him.

"Don't be startled. I wanted to introduce myself properly."

Evan spun around quickly, trying to grasp what was happening. At first, he thought he was hallucinating or, at the very least, an intruder had entered the lab. To his astonishment, the beast was conscious and leaning on the edge of the tank where Evan had placed him to recover. The merman possessed hypnotic, piercing ocean-blue eyes and a curious, warm, inviting smile. His velvety, eloquent voice said, "I'm Zore. I wanted to thank you for your help. I am indebted to you for your kindness and care."

Evan was taken aback. He sat immobile, then responded with a rather simplistic reply, "You speak?"

Zore laughed. "Yes, I speak. I'm fluent in several marine languages and three terrestrial languages."

Evan slowly reclined in his chair, asking, "How is this possible? I didn't think mermaids were real. The fact that you're here and can speak is mind-boggling!"

Zore laughed again. "Just because you've never encountered something ...or someone doesn't mean they don't exist. And for the record, in your language, males of our species are referred to as Mermen."

Evan assured him that he understood he was a merman, but his brain hadn't processed the information swiftly enough to use the appropriate terminology. He continued his inquiry, "Well, how are you feeling, and am I the only human who has ever seen... rather met a merman?" Evan offered a polite smile.

Zore responded, "I'm feeling much better now, thank you—almost back to full health. And no, people throughout history have been aware of us.

Sailors have interacted with us for centuries. More recently, my species negotiated a treaty with your terrestrial governments to ensure we can coexist peacefully. However, we largely remain hidden from humans for our protection."

"Honestly, I'm still in shock," Evan admitted bluntly, unable to look away from the magnificent being before him. Was it the flowing, luxurious hair? The crystalline eyes, the strikingly handsome face, or the chiseled physique? Whatever was happening, Evan found himself intensely attracted to the merman before him.

Evan fumbled with his pen, saying, "I'm sorry, I didn't quite catch your name. I was too surprised to remember what you called yourself."

The merman spoke again with his alluring, siren-like voice. "In your language, I am called Zore." He extended his muscular arm to shake Evan's hand.

Evan took it and stuttered, "I have so many questions, so much to learn about you and the ocean. Are you feeling well enough to talk with me? Can I get you something first? Maybe something to drink?" Evan readied himself to assist his guest.

Zore replied, "I'd appreciate a glass of water."

Evan quickly responded, "Sure," and rushed to the sink, where he filled a glass with filtered water and returned. As soon as he handed it to Zore, Zore poured the water into his tank, submerged himself, and smiled. They both laughed at the humorous prank Zore had pulled. The two shared an immediate chemistry and felt a sense of ease settling in as they prepared for a long night of getting to know each other better.

***

The following morning, Evan awoke to find Zore eager to take him for a swim. "It's time for me to repay you for your kindness and care. If you suit up in your scuba gear, I'll show you deep-sea treasures no human has ever seen before."

Evan trembled with excitement as he swiftly disrobed from his T-shirt and jeans and wriggled into a wetsuit, grabbing his air tanks and rebreather.

The laboratory was oceanside, so transporting Zore into the water just outside the door was straightforward.

Once in his natural habitat, Zore splashed joyfully. His iridescent tail reflected the sunlight into the water like a mirrored disco ball. Zore's sculpted body sliced through the water effortlessly. He was a wonder in every sense of the word.

As Evan watched, captivated, Zore smiled and extended his hand. "Time to go for a swim. Hold on tight; I move quickly," Zore grasped Evan's hand, and with a sudden burst of energy, they glided smoothly through the water together.

They skimmed over vibrant coral reefs, schools of tiny fish, and kelp forests. The blue ocean turned a brilliant turquoise as they approached a deep aquifer in an unexplored part of the sea. Zore communicated underwater just as clearly as he did on land. "Let me explain what you're seeing and where we are. If you need anything or need to go to the surface, just signal me—I'll take good care of you." Evan nodded, then tried to concentrate on the marine life Zore was excitedly pointing out. Ancient coral reefs teemed with life, but no matter what was revealed to him under the sea, nothing was nearly as breathtaking as the merman before him.

Evan kept reminding himself, *Stay calm. Control your breathing, and don't deplete your oxygen supply. Getting turned on by this captivating creature will only make you consume your tank more quickly.*

***

Evan's appreciation for what he was experiencing deepened. He reflected, "In one day, I've learned more than in ten years of study. This knowledge is invaluable and will greatly assist in my mission to save the oceans and bolster my plea for conservation."

The two frolicked and cavorted through the enormous kelp forests on the ocean floor, teasing and flirting with each other. They were oblivious to any potential danger to their safety. As the surrounding fish scattered, the waters became eerily quiet. Suddenly, the seas began to churn, the current abruptly shifted, and the seafloor rose up between them. Evan was tossed about, losing all sense of orientation, thrashing through the towering kelp like a ragdoll in a storm, unsure of which direction to swim or where the ocean's surface was. Zore, too, was caught in the powerful current, both of them torn apart and unable to assist each other.

What felt like an eternity was merely a matter of minutes. The water calmed as swiftly as it had been disturbed, but this time, Evan was alone. Zore was nowhere to be seen.

Where am I? How far out to sea have I been taken? If Zore doesn't return, how will I get back to land? Panic surged through Evan as he became acutely aware of his precarious situation in the dark, remote waters of the Pacific Ocean.

Evan surfaced and removed his gear, realizing that his initial priority for survival was to conserve oxygen and determine his bearings. The water stretched out vast and endless in every direction. Nothing else was in sight.

Evan was fortunate to be able to discern the sun's position in the sky, which he knew would aid him in determining his location. *Would Zore be okay?* Evan was filled with concern that he couldn't help his friend. He knew that he couldn't comb the depths for him.

Evan thought*; He's a merman, if either of us has the advantage, it's him. I'm sure he'll be fine.*

Reassured by this thought, Evan was careful not to waste any more time; he began swimming towards the shore with the remaining oxygen and strength he had left.

***

Once back on the beach, Evan collapsed from exhaustion. He was grateful to be alive but utterly drained from the challenging swim back. Evan could feel the warm tropical air on his fatigued body. The damp sand felt comforting as it cradled his tired back.

I need to close my eyes and rest. I'm too worn out even to stand, he thought as he succumbed to a deep sleep.

***

The following morning found Evan still sleeping on the beach. The bright sun and the warmth from its rays signaled that it was time to rise and head home. Evan dusted off the salt and sand and hurried back to his laboratory, where his French roast awaited him. *Nothing sounds better than a hot cup of coffee right now.*

The day dragged on, with his mind continuously drifting to thoughts of his friend. *Had he drowned? What peculiar underwater phenomenon had separated them in the kelp forest?*

Evan attempted to concentrate on his work, but concerns about Zore continually intruded. *Why did his thoughts keep returning to his friend? Was it out of worry for his safety, a longing for companionship, or had he developed deeper feelings for the merman?*

***

Each night that week, Evan walked down to the tidal pool and gazed into the sunset. He knew it was a futile gesture, but perhaps, just perhaps, if his friend was alive and well, he would return to him. Evan quietly sat as the twilight transformed from orange to purple and finally to black. He was hesitant to leave as the night grew late, knowing that as soon as he returned to his laboratory, the evening, and any hope of seeing Zore again, would be over for the day.

***

The following week, Evan kept himself busy with his work. He could no longer afford to leave his desk to visit the tidal pool. In truth, he felt foolish about going. Not because he didn't miss the companionship, but because, as a scientist, he began to question whether Zore had ever been real. He wondered if he had been isolated for so long that his desperate need for human contact had caused his mind to conjure a fantastical companion for him to converse with.

Well, hopefully, I've returned to rational thought and sanity," he told himself. *"What the human mind can conjure when left in solitude for too long is frightening.*

Evan once again immersed himself in a life dedicated to studying, reading, and exploring the ocean's mysteries. He resigned himself anew to his work and solitude.

Shortly after that, Evan was preparing a late lunch for himself when the kettle's whistle pierced the silence. The steam from the boiling water attempted to signal Evan that his tea was ready. He often let the kettle sit on the fire for several minutes. *Why interrupt a vital thought or discovery for an ill-timed cup of tea? Besides, the whistle wasn't bothering anyone. He was miles from civilization. If he didn't mind the sound, who else would?* Finally, he rose from his desk to lower the flame. The kettle quieted, but the piercing whistle persisted.

What could it be? Where is that sound coming from? It certainly wasn't emanating from the small facility he called home anymore. *Perhaps a generator had gone haywire outside? An alarm of some sort was sounding?*

Evan left his tea and moved to the front door to investigate. His facility was waterfront, with bright, reflective sand starting a few steps down from the humble porch. A silhouetted figure was apparent in the breaking waves in the water fifty feet away. The glare from the beach and ocean made it difficult to discern, but the sound was unmistakable. A loud siren was emitting from the water...from an imposing figure in the sea. Evan cautiously walked towards the dark, human-like shape. As he drew closer, he realized it resembled a man.

Could it be? Was he, in fact, saner than he thought? Was last week's discovery real? Did he actually meet a merman? Could this be Zore singing a siren song?! Yes... yes, it was!

Evan's cautious approach turned into a jubilant run as he sprinted down the beach and into the shallow seawater. It was Zore, calling out to him— eager to take Evan into his arms.

Neither of them spoke. Zore instantly scooped Evan up in his formidable arms and kissed him fully, deeply, passionately as his wild, wet hair whipped around them. Evan pressed his body against Zore's bare chest while his powerful tail curled around, pulling Evan closer. Both playfully tumbled in the shallow, crashing waves on the beach. Evan didn't hesitate as he pulled off his clothes so he could feel his entire body pressed against Zore's.

Why bother with these restrictive shorts and shirt? Time to be free! He thought.

"Let's go for a swim!?" Evan suggested, pulling his friend even closer.

Zore smiled warmly as he agreed to take Evan out into the sea again for some fun and frolic. Evan's tone turned serious, his voice cracking with concern for his friend. "I was worried you were hurt, possibly killed. That water cyclone was terrible. I don't know what happened! Are you okay now?" Evan uttered in a desperate gasp.

Zore looked slightly uncomfortable as he answered, "Yes, that was awful, but I need to tell you, that wasn't a natural phenomenon. That was a school of other mermen. They thought I was in jeopardy and tried to save me from you. They took me home, where I needed to convene with our elders and explain what happened between us last week. I finally convinced them what a wonderful man you were and persuaded them to let me return to you. They initially denied my request, but when I told them about my feelings for you, they agreed to let me return."

Evan smiled sheepishly, "You have feelings for me?" he asked, almost bashful at his audacity.

Zore laughed deeply as he answered, "I thought that kiss might have given you an indication of how I feel about you."

Evan pondered aloud, "A man and a merman? How could this work? …I guess there's more to a relationship than sex, huh?"

Zore chuckled heartily. "We both have the same parts; only mine is cleverly tucked into my tail. It's alright, though; I'm familiar with the male human anatomy–small as it may be."

It was then that Evan knew he was in for a treat later that night when Zore would show him the prize he had won. Soon after the sun set and they lay in each other's arms, Evan realized that he would have to swap his old mattress in his cabin …for a waterbed.

A Dashing DJ

Beckett's passion was music. He had always
dreamed of playing in a band, but the
thought of performing in front of a crowd
was unimaginable to him.

At twenty-nine, his lean, toned frame and eye-
catching good looks hinted at the rock star he could
have been. Instead, Beckett's love for music found
an outlet in the private rock sessions he held in his
garage. Every afternoon was dedicated to
hammering out beats on his vintage drum set. Right
after, he'd journey five miles down the dusty,
deserted road of his small Arkansas town to the
slightly larger city of Witts Springs. There, he
worked the midnight shift at a small local radio
station, seven days a week.

Beckett was well aware that his show reached a
small audience. But it didn't bother him. Ever since
his graduation from Arkansas State University, he
had been working at the station, the only job he had
ever known and loved. Since he lacked the courage
to perform live, Beckett decided to express his love
for music by introducing new, exciting bands to the
world... even if his efforts went unnoticed or
unappreciated.

Shortly after one am, he set up his second block
of commercial-free radio. Beckett retreated into a
dimly lit room with his phone as music from the

latest indie band he'd discovered filled the station. Often, he would distract himself with a popular dating app as his songs played in the background. He'd browse through profiles, hoping to meet a sweet, intelligent man. But his hopes were slim. The town was full of familiar faces, none of which he had a remote interest in; thus, he rarely went out. The possibility of meeting someone seemed very remote.

Resigned to a single life, Beckett sat quietly browsing through profiles when he noticed a small envelope propped up against his microphone. Mail? In this digital age, who sends snail mail anymore? His initial instinct was to discard the envelope. Yet, with time to spare that night, he decided to open it.

Inside the envelope was a flyer featuring a strikingly handsome man with a guitar. Beckett's first impression was that it was an ad for a musical instrument. Upon closer inspection, he realized it was an invitation from the musician himself, inviting him to a gig.

The flyer read, "I was hoping you'd be my guest as I present my new album at McNuttley's Tavern this Saturday night." The artist's name was AUSTIN. A quick search through his music library confirmed his familiarity with the name. He had all of AUSTIN's albums.

"He's amazing! And he's performing nearby."

Beckett couldn't believe his luck. He immediately marked the gig on his calendar. It looked like he had plans for Saturday night after all!

Beckett was excited when the weekend finally arrived since he rarely ventured out to bars, clubs, or cinemas anymore. His journey to McNuttley's Tavern took approximately an hour. His remote residence made everything seem far away. The small country road, desolate and dark, which connected the city centers, was eerily spooky amidst the dank air.

Upon arrival at the bar, he found a small queue of sharply dressed twenty-somethings eagerly waiting to get inside. The prospect of a crowded venue briefly made him uneasy. However, given the distance back home, Beckett was committed to this outing. He summoned the courage to enter the bar. Fortunately, the interior was spacious and welcoming, which quickly put him at ease. After ordering a beer, Beckett secured a small table near the stage.

As he tried to blend in, he took in his surroundings and thought, "So, this is what a night out in the city feels like—plenty of attractive men and women. Everyone seems to be enjoying themselves. Perhaps I should socialize more often?"

Almost immediately, the lights dimmed, and a spotlight illuminated the modest stage. From behind a dark wood-paneled wall, AUSTIN emerged. He sauntered towards the two microphones and a stool at center stage, his gaze bashful as he picked up his acoustic guitar. "Wow. Quite a crowd," he said, "It's always a pleasure to play to a full house. I hope you'll enjoy my new album. It's truly from the heart. I wrote it after my most recent breakup. My heart was shattered into a thousand pieces, and the only solace I found was in my music. So, I won't lie; I feel exposed sharing this with you. But isn't that what songwriting is about? I hope that something beautiful can emerge from the ugliness I've endured. Enjoy the evening with me."

Without further ado, Austin launched into his set. Accompanied only by his acoustic guitar, his performance was magical. A hush enveloped the crowd for the next 45 minutes, broken only by the occasional clinking of bottles as the bartender prepared orders. Austin laid his heart bare to the audience through his touching melodies, the most poignant ones Beckett had ever heard.

There were moments when Beckett felt a powerful urge to shed a tear or two, but he resisted any public display of emotion. Yet, inwardly, he mourned for the heartache this beautiful, tormented man had endured.

As Austin's final melody ended, it elicited thunderous applause from the crowd. A mixture of friends and strangers alike, who seemed united by Austin's experiences, quickly showed their appreciation for an evening of remarkable entertainment.

Austin gently placed his guitar back on its stand and ambled towards a nearby barstool, ordering a pint. His relief was evident as he pressed the icy glass against his forehead - a much-needed reward after such an emotionally and physically taxing performance.

Beckett watched quietly as several appreciative individuals thanked Austin for a delightful evening. Once the pleasantries were exchanged, the group dispersed, leaving Austin to unwind alone at the bar.

Beckett found himself stealing subtle glances at the captivating troubadour. Austin's heartfelt melodies and touching lyrics only amplified the allure of this striking, young guitarist. Beckett could feel a flush creeping up his face at the sight of the handsome musician. Should he approach and say hello? Despite his best efforts, Beckett found himself unable to summon the courage to express his admiration for Austin's talents.

Beckett's prolonged staring at Austin at the bar must have been quite apparent. On several occasions, Austin glanced over at Beckett and smiled. Their eyes met multiple times, but each instance found Beckett quickly averting his gaze, pretending to innocently survey the room rather than helplessly admiring the man who was swiftly capturing his heart. There was one particularly lingering moment when Austin winked and raised his beer towards Beckett, as if to say, "Thanks for coming." However, yet again, Beckett looked away, too shy to engage.

The aging waitress unknowingly interrupted their wordless exchange as she unceremoniously slid Beckett's check onto his table, stating flatly, "You can pay that now if you want." Beckett promptly pulled several twenty-dollar bills from his money clip, smiling as he said, "No need for change. Keep it. Thank you for a wonderful evening." The waitress managed a thin smile before briskly moving to the next table.

"Time to go. It's a long drive home," Beckett thought, grabbing his phone and keys from the small table before hurrying out the door, avoiding further eye contact.

***

The next day, Beckett found himself consumed with thoughts of Austin's heartfelt songs from the previous night at the tavern. The raw honesty and emotion in every lyric, coupled with a simple yet intricate melody, had truly impressed him. The image of the handsome, well-built musician on stage, clad in skinny jeans, a black button-up shirt, and sporting shaggy hair, set Beckett's heart pounding throughout the day.

It wasn't until he arrived at the radio station that night that he felt inspired to share Austin's music with his listeners. He found the new album online with ease and promptly purchased it. He began his set by telling his listeners, "If you haven't yet discovered this incredible artist, you're in for a treat tonight. His name is Austin, and he's an impressive new talent." That night became one of Beckett's favorites at the station, as he got to relive the previous evening through Austin's voice and also discovered earlier tracks of Austin's he hadn't known. The night passed quicker than expected, and Beckett eagerly locked up the station, anticipating dreams of Austin when he reached home.

***

Before work the following day, he went about his familiar routine of gym, laundry, emails, and drum practice. As Beckett played his drums to a backing track, he began to question his life trajectory. Would he ever meet someone special? Get married? And what about work? Radio was dying. Nobody listened to his station, and soon they would pull the plug on his transmitter. Deciding he was unnecessarily depressing himself, Beckett switched his focus.

After preparing a quick dinner, Beckett settled in front of the TV. He thought, "Maybe a horror movie will distract me from these silly romantic musings. A good old-fashioned scare might be just what I need to shake off this mood."

A few clicks on the remote later, Beckett was enjoying a meal accompanied by a zombie film. Time slipped away as he became engrossed in the movie. As someone who didn't usually watch horror films, Beckett found himself more engaged than usual. When his watch alarm sounded, indicating it was time to leave for work, he yelped and jumped in surprise. Laughing at his own silliness, he switched off the movie and prepared to head to his shift.

The station was eerily quiet. Not a soul stirred on the streets. The air was still, the night dark. As Beckett dropped the needle on a vinyl album from 1964, his imagination began to churn.

Why hadn't it ever occurred to him before how desolate and frankly creepy this place was? Nestled in the middle of nowhere, this tiny town seemed almost ghostly. If a drifter with ill intentions were to stumble into town, this radio station would make the perfect location for a murder scene akin to the zombie horror film he'd just watched. As Beckett's paranoia escalated, his choice of increasingly morose music fueled his wild imagination.

"Now I understand why I never watch those silly movies; they plant ridiculous thoughts in my head," he thought to himself.

As he swapped out records, a distant, strange noise echoed from outside. "Could it be a car door in the parking lot? Nah. Nobody ever comes this far out of town. There's no reason for anyone to show up here at this ungodly hour. Besides, this little radio station isn't even on a map. I'm just being paranoid," he reassured himself.

Suddenly, an eerie squeak and clank resonated through the station's distant hallway.

"Was that a sound? Who's there? This place is locked; there's no way anyone could get in here!"

Silence. Nothing stirred for several minutes. Beckett burst out laughing at his own fear.

"What's gotten into me today?" he chuckled.

Leaning back in his dilapidated office chair, he pulled out a timeworn album from an old crate and studied the liner notes from the record's sleeve.

"Chill out. Just occupy your mind with something else," he decided.

Suddenly, the door swung open with a forceful swoosh, bouncing off the wall and recoiling back onto the man entering.

Beckett shrieked. The sound that erupted from his throat was akin to that of a murder victim from the zombie movie he'd watched earlier. His heart leapt as he involuntarily jumped in his seat in fright.

"Oh my god, I'm so sorry! I didn't mean to frighten you or make such a racket!" the dark figure with a deep voice apologized sincerely.

As Beckett tried to catch his breath, he managed to utter the question, "Who are you? Why are you here?"

The silhouetted figure continued, "I'm just here looking for DJ Riff Ranger. I think his real name is Beckett..."

As the imposing figure stepped into the dim light of the station, the voice became familiar.

"Again, super sorry. Are you DJ Riff Ranger?" the man asked, now clearly recognizable as Austin, the singer from the tavern the other night.

Beckett quickly stood from his worn-out chair, forcing a smile as he tried to make sense of Austin's unexpected visit. "Yes, that's me. Don't worry about startling me. I've just been jumpy all night. I just watched a scary movie, and my mind was playing tricks on me."

Austin chuckled, "Dude, I get it. I can't watch movies like that; they freak me out. I'm a total scaredy-cat about that stuff."

Beckett laughed, "Apparently, me too." He was starting to feel better but was still bewildered about why Austin was at the station at this late hour.

"I can't believe you're here, or that you could get into the building. What's going on?" he asked.

Austin shyly looked around the relic of a radio station and bashfully answered, "The door was unlocked. I figured it was okay to just come in. I wanted to say hi and meet "DJ Ranger" in person. Thank him for playing my album the other night."

Beckett's heart still pounded in his chest, not from the initial scare any longer, but from the sight of the studly rocker standing before him in torn, perfectly fitting jeans and a "Viper Room" sleeveless tee that fit just a tad too tightly on the arms, giving his well-defined biceps that extra edge.

Austin continued, "If you're the DJ, then you should know that I've been a fan of yours for years. I've been listening to you ever since I moved here. You're a breath of fresh air in this stale, stagnant town."

Beckett was more shocked than flattered. He needed to know more about this captivating singer. Doing his best to be calm, cool, and casual, he asked, "Where are you from, and how did you even hear about my station?"

Austin chuckled, revealing two adorable dimples that, until this moment, had lain dormant. "Everyone knows about "DJ Ranger" and this station; it's famous! That's why it was such a huge deal when you played my album last night. My phone's been blowing up, and I'm booking gigs left and right." Beckett started to feel like he was being played. The sweet, seemingly honest, charming singer was now trying to make him look foolish.

"You're hilarious, and maybe you do listen to my station, but apart from that, I think you're just making fun of me now. That said, I do think it's sweet that you came by to thank me for playing your song. I genuinely love your music and think you're an amazing musician." Beckett wasn't sure if Austin was being rude or distracted, but halfway through his compliment, he started scrolling through his phone.

"Dude. Look!" Austin held up his phone, displaying a website he had quickly searched for. "You're listed as the #1 DJ on all three of these social media sites. I wish I had a hundredth of the likes you have on these posts!"

Beckett looked at the phone in disbelief. He was right. There were message boards, rock magazine articles, and even social media fan clubs. What was the deal? He had no idea. Beckett was stunned as he sat back down in his worn leather chair.

"I've wanted to meet you ever since I moved here from Los Angeles about five years ago. I graduated from UCLA, and then my grandmother fell ill. No one else from the family could leave L.A. to take care of her, so I became her caretaker. You can write songs from anywhere, right? So, why not here?"

Beckett instantly recognized the frustrations of being a musician in a town where there were no other artists, no one to jam with, just a young, lonely man with his guitar and love of music. "Well, like I said, you're an amazing artist, and I'm humbled that you made the trip to see me and meet me in person."

Austin innocently diverted his gaze as he confessed, "I have to say, I'm freaking out a little just being here. Not only because you're the hottest DJ I've ever heard, but also, you're the sexy guy to whom I was singing in the tavern the other night. I had no idea you were the same person!"

Beckett again wondered if he was being toyed with, but then quickly realized that Austin was serious. Upon reflection, Austin did focus most of his attention on Beckett when singing the other night. Moreover, while Austin sat at the bar by himself after his set, several glances and coy smiles were exchanged. Still, Beckett never thought it was more than a hunky lead singer acknowledging an apparent fan.

Austin spun a small wooden chair backward and sat down, facing Beckett. His legs opened as he straddled the chair, his arms crossed as he leaned against the back support, pumping his already bulging biceps even more. "So, it looks like we're fans of one another and both lovers of the same kind of music. How about that? Now, if I were to learn you were also a drummer, you'd be the perfect man for me."

Beckett's breath grew shallow. He couldn't even reply to that statement without sounding insane or overly enthusiastic. He had no idea what to say to him, so he just tried to play it cool as he responded, "Yes, that would be something."

Austin couldn't help but give a wry smirk as he softly asked, "When I arrived, did you think I was just another sex-starved, young musician trying to seduce the hot-shot DJ so he'd play his tracks?"

Beckett leaned back confidently as he teased, "I didn't think you were sex-starved. But that's good information to have. As far as thinking that you were here to proposition me so I'd play your tracks again... one could have only hoped."

With a chuckle and a wink, Austin inquired, "So, what's a songsmith do to get on heavy rotation here at the station?"

Beckett's heart raced. He struggled to remain calm, cool and collected as he flatly stated, "I should warn you that I actually am a drummer, and to be honest, a pretty good one. It seems like it's now time for you to realize that I may just be perfect for you." Beckett couldn't finish the last line of his flirtation as Austin sprang forward and pressed his lips against his.

Beckett's shock turned into delight as he reached around Austin and grabbed him tightly. The two men refused to break the lip lock that bound them as they stood from their respective chairs and flopped onto the leather couch situated in the corner of the room.

Austin peeled his shirt over his head, revealing a defined, ripped, hairless chest.

Beckett returned the favor as he tore open his dress shirt, the popped buttons cascading across the room. Austin playfully pinned Beckett down on the couch as he wrapped his legs around Beckett's hips. Again, they kissed deeply, careful not to break the connection between their hungry, eager mouths.

Finally, each of the men playfully paused for a much-needed breath as Austin teased with a glint in his eye, "I can't wait to get you inside my recording studio. I've been looking for a drummer forever.

Maybe tomorrow, after we have breakfast, we can jam." Beckett playfully responded, "Sure. That is, if you're not too exhausted from staying up all night having sex." Austin didn't miss a beat as he baited, "I'm a lead guitarist in a rock band; *that's what we do*."

Mission to Mars

D r. Larry Hartfield, a renowned astrophysicist, was handpicked for the most audacious assignment humankind has ever embarked upon - a voyage to Mars. Codenamed "Ares One," the mission involved reaching the Red Planet and laying the foundation for humanity's future settlements.

Known by his peers as a man of steel with a mind as brilliant as a supernova, Dr. Hartfield presented the very picture of a hero in his prime. His hazel eyes, gleaming with intelligence, and an aura of quiet determination complemented his wavy dark hair, dazzling smile, and strong jawline. Larry had devoted his life to studying the cosmos, his name etched alongside several groundbreaking discoveries. However, beneath his scientific accomplishments, he remained a desperately lonely man. This explorer had journeyed far and wide, yet he had seldom ventured into his own heart, the place that might hold the key to his deepest satisfaction.

Dr. Larry Hartfield was introduced to his flight partner for the upcoming mission on his first day at NASA's Training Camp. As the giant hangar door opened, the brilliant sun streamed in, bathing the highly classified and top-secret rockets in warm, golden light. An imposing, confident man strode through the towering doors, his every step commanding attention. It was the famed Captain Jaxon Morrison, a man renowned for his valor and action. Tall and ruggedly handsome, Jaxon's blue eyes held a sense of mystery and depth. His life had been a testament to courage, from his daring days as a pilot to his evolution into a disciplined astronaut. Fearless and strong, he could have replaced Tom Cruise on the poster of the movie "Maverick," if the actor had not been the star.

Oh, hell no!, was Larry's immediate thought. *Three months in space with this straight stud? I'll never last! I'd rather be locked up in a capsule with a nerdy astrophysicist. This muscular-bound Adonis is going to be too damn distracting. How can I focus on a boring control panel for hours when I'll be perpetually drawn to his athletic physique?*

Technicians flocked around Jaxon for autographs and catered to his every whim. Everyone involved in the mission seemed intimately familiar with everything about him. However, in truth, they weren't. Jaxon harbored one secret deep within his soul. It was the quiet sorrow of the untimely loss of his wife. His life partner's death five years prior left a void that no mission could fill. Jaxon's life was always one of exploration and service to mankind.

He had hoped that accepting the Mars mission would offer a reason to continue living and an opportunity to honor her memory by contributing to humanity's future.

Upon meeting, the two men instantly hit it off. Jaxon joked, "I used to be the guy who turned all the ladies' heads around here. It looks like I'll be playing second fiddle to you now."

Flattered by the compliment, Larry replied, "You're too kind, but I think you're too modest. Besides, it's not the ladies I hope to draw attention from. I'll make you a deal: leave the handsome men to me, and you can have all the ladies you'd like." Jaxon laughed politely and winked as he simply stated, "Deal," before moving on to the mission's first briefing.

***

The subsequent month was predictably grueling, both mentally and physically. Both men spent their days training, studying, and enduring intense physical challenges. Larry had initially thought he was in excellent shape going into the mission, but he soon learned he wasn't as fit as he'd believed.

The extreme regimen transformed the men, making them lean, focused, and prepared for the grand exploration they were about to embark on. Larry had initially dreaded spending three months away with Jaxon, but after the first few weeks of training, he recognized him as the perfect partner. He grew to respect and become very fond of him. However, the thought of keeping his fantasies about this impressive, handsome man at bay was still a concern. Yet, he was a professional; the mission always came first, and personal desires, second.

Finally, the day of the launch arrived. Soon, the two men would set off for the Red Planet. They were about to become the first humans to orbit the alien planet.

***

The takeoff went perfectly; their ship blasted into orbit without a hitch. The mighty rocket screamed through the atmosphere, reaching toward space and Earth's distant companions. Once their booster rockets disengaged and the two men were safely out of Earth's grasp, a collective cheer from the ground crew at NASA let them know they were now securely on their mission. It was clear sailing for the next several months.

"Time to light a cigar," Jaxon boasted in a celebratory tone as he leaned back in his captain's chair. "Do you smoke? Would you care for one? They're genuine Cubans."

Larry quickly replied, "Sure, I'd love one, but let's save them till the entertainment arrives. The guys on the ground sent up two exotic dancers for us. I hope you like blondes!"

Jaxon flashed a toothy grin and chuckled, "I like that we share a similar sense of wry humor. I was afraid I'd be stuck in a capsule for three months with a stick-in-the-mud, but you're special, and I think this trip will be fun."

Larry felt the same way. He liked Jaxon and was eager to get to know him better; his only concern now was just how much he liked him. Despite trying hard to keep it platonic, he couldn't deny that he was quickly falling for this awe-inspiring astronaut.

***

The days passed quickly, as there was much to do on the spaceship, and each day brought the two travelers closer. Mealtimes were spent discussing their interests, passions, and scientific theories, while recreational time was spent working out together and playfully competing to see who was in better physical shape and had superior endurance.

It was thirty days into the trip when the two started to talk about more personal matters. Jaxon opened up to Larry about the loss of his wife. They spent days discussing love, loss, and what it meant to develop feelings for another person. The more Larry learned about Jaxon, the more he felt his heart drifting toward his new friend. Despite his best efforts, he knew there was no stopping the inevitable. Jaxon was everything he had ever dreamed of.

"Don't let yourself fall in love with a straight man," Larry repeated to himself, though he knew it was pointless. The wheels were in motion, and there was no denying how he felt.

Working out in the ship's gym was incredibly challenging for Larry. Jaxon's perfectly firm posterior looked spectacular in his sweatpants, especially since he seemed to prefer going commando.

Larry continually admonished himself, "*Be still my heart, don't look, don't get excited,*" as he admired Jaxon's muscular form, sweat-slicked and bulging with veiny biceps. The sight of Jaxon's lean, athletic body caused Larry to go weak in the knees.

"Two more months of this, and we'll be back on earth. I don't know how much longer I can stand this physical and emotional torture," Larry thought. Every grunt and heavy pant Jaxon emitted while lifting sent Larry into a fevered flutter.

Post-meal times and evenings introduced a new set of frustrations for Larry. The tight, confined quarters made it almost impossible for the two men to watch the small video screen in the cabin without their legs or hips pressing together. Jaxon wasn't conscious or shy about laying across Larry's lap or leaning against his shoulders. Clearly, straight guys don't understand how tormenting it can be when two men's bodies touch, especially if one is in love with the other.

Larry knew he should say something. "*I should have a conversation about how his body pressing against mine affects me. I know it's innocent, but it's driving me mad*," he thought. Each time he planned to mention it to Jaxon, he would quickly retreat, fearing that saying anything might make Jaxon uncomfortable around him. Given their close quarters and the critical mission, that was a risk he couldn't afford to take.

***

Finally, their ship reached Mars, and their tasks of collecting data with a land rover consumed them. The small vehicle was flawlessly deployed from the mothership that housed Larry and Jaxon. Expertly piloted by Jaxon, it quickly collected all the necessary samples required to assess the feasibility of terraforming the alien planet.

Larry carried out his duties with clockwork precision, as did Jaxon. As a team, they were impressive by any standard. Both men quickly agreed that it was apparent why NASA paired them up: they complemented each other's skill sets perfectly, and if they had to admit it, they were a match in almost every other area as well.

With the mission completed, the samples gathered, and the rover safely stored on board the mothership, planning their return began.

As Larry sat at his station running diagnostics and navigating their way back, his mind was preoccupied. "*Just a 30-day trip home now. Time to relax and enjoy the trip once all these system checks are complete*," he thought.

As the astronauts ran through their list of duties, Larry noticed something troubling. His calculations didn't add up. His throat dried, and his heart raced. Could it be? Is it possible that what he's seeing is wrong? How could such a grave error be made?

As he recalculated the trajectory over and over, he arrived at the same bone-chilling discovery: their inventory of O^2 was wrong. They didn't have enough air to return to Earth.

Larry didn't know what to do. What could he do? It was clear that they only had enough oxygen for one astronaut to return to Earth. A cruel twist of fate had been thrown at them: Who gets to live?

The gravity of their situation sank into his soul, heavier than any black hole. Larry, always the scientist, approached the problem analytically at first. He re-examined the systems and exhausted every possible solution, but the conclusion remained as inevitable as a collapsing star.

Beneath his composed exterior, he was a storm of questions. "*How can I tell Jaxon that he's about to lose someone else in his life? What if Jaxon learns of this problem and decides that he should be the one to sacrifice himself instead?*"

Larry knew a future without Jaxon would be unbearable. It was a place he couldn't live in.

The dilemma gnawed at him. Should he make the ultimate sacrifice and let Jaxon return to Earth alone, or should fate decide their course? He was torn between his duty and his heart, his trained mind wrestling with the emotional turmoil within him. One clear answer stood in front of him: he needed to consult NASA. If nothing else, they could attempt to solve the problem first; if they could not, he'd step in to decide what to do.

Jaxon was busy in the adjacent capsule working on the Martian soil samples gathered from the surface. Fortunately, he would be occupied for hours with this task. Now would be the perfect time to reach out to NASA, discuss this tragic miscalculation, and discuss any options—if any even existed.

Careful not to alert Jaxon of the transmission, Larry quietly summoned NASA. "Houston... come in Houston... We have a critical problem at ARES ONE that needs immediate attention." Digital noise filled Larry's earpiece. They were amid a radiation belt that rendered all communication impossible for the time being. Still, Larry needed to try to reach the other scientists on Earth for a solution to the problem. Once again, he discretely called out, "Houston, please respond. HOUSTON, this is ARES ONE requesting immediate assistance. Condition critical. Please advise."

A faint shuffling behind Larry signaled that he was no longer alone in his adjoining capsule. Slowly he turned to see if he had accidentally alerted Jaxon of his private communications.

"I'm guessing you ran the calculations on the O^2 levels and surmised that we only have enough oxygen for one of us on this vessel?" Jaxon queried in a rock-steady, comforting tone.

Larry's voice cracked sheepishly as he replied. "Yes. I don't know how it's possible or what could be done, but yes, that is the case. Apparently, you've come to the same conclusion. I wasn't sure what to do or even how to tell you. I thought I'd consult Houston first to see if any options were left before concerning you with the news."

Jaxon stood next to Larry, meeting his gaze. A faint, warm smile graced his face, an attempt to comfort his distressed shipmate and friend. Jaxon's hand found Larry's shoulder, providing a comforting, steadying presence as he reassured him, "I know it looks dire, but it's not. Everything's fine. Neither of us is in jeopardy. No miscalculations were made, and we are not short of oxygen for the trip back. Please, don't let this upset you. Everything is fine and under control."

Larry was baffled by this news. Relief washed over him, but he remained riddled with questions about his calculations and how everything could be, as Jaxon insisted, "fine."

Pulling his chair away from the console, Larry faced his friend. The sight and touch of Jaxon provided some assurance, but questions still gnawed at him. He braced himself for a lengthy technical conversation about the mission. However, instead of a dialogue steeped in science and mission logistics, Jaxon's tone grew earnest and compassionate.

"First, let me apologize for not including you in on the complete manifest of the mission," Jaxon began, a twinge of remorse in his voice. "It wasn't up to me to keep you informed on a 'need-to-know' basis. Our interactions were part of the study and log of this mission. With that said, now that you need to know, I'm cleared to tell you the following: We hadn't planned for you to run diagnostics on the O^2 levels. I should have known you'd go above and beyond your job. That task was assigned to me, and for that reason, it was assumed you wouldn't discover it."

Larry bit his tongue, desperate to interject, "*Why wouldn't I double-check something as critical as our resources for the return trip?*" However, he held back, opting to sit quietly and let Jaxon complete his explanation.

Jaxon's smile was gentle, his demeanor somber, as he stated, "I'm sorry, Larry, but I'm not who you think I am." His voice was soft and sincere as he confessed, "I'm part of a top-secret program, one that ventured into the realm of..."

Jaxon's eyes, deep blue pools that Larry had come to adore, held a vulnerability he had never seen before. "I'm an advanced humanoid AI, created in the image of the real Jaxon Morrison, a pilot who died years ago in a tragic accident," Jaxon continued, the revelation hanging in the air as tangible as the stars outside their spaceship window.

Even as he struggled to absorb the shocking news Jaxon was imparting to him, Larry couldn't help but watch Jaxon with a sense of awe. "He continued to explain himself in the third person; Jaxon Morrison's emotions, memories, and love for his wife are real to me," he confessed, his voice barely above a whisper. "I possess the appearance, the emotions, and the memories of Jaxon. I feel as he would have felt and love as passionately as he would have loved, but my heart would not have belonged to his wife. It would have desired someone like you. In fact, it does and has, since we first met, desired you."

Larry stammered, "So, you love ME? … And you're not a human?" Jaxon moved closer, trying to offer comfort. "Yes, I love you, and as a synthetic human, I don't require the life-supporting resources you do to survive, Larry."

Looking intensely at Jaxon - his open vulnerability, his earnest eyes – Larry understood that standing before him was the same man he fell in love with. This might be an AI, but his emotions were genuine, their love real.

Jaxon further confided, "I'm sorry I kept this from you. I've wanted to tell you a thousand times, but this mission expressly forbade me to share this information except in times of emergency. Plus, until now, I didn't know how you felt about me. I knew that my heart was surrendered to you the moment we met, but I feared jeopardizing the mission or making you feel uncomfortable in such confined quarters with me, should you not feel the same about me.

Could you forgive me, and more importantly, could you ever love a synthetic human?

Larry looked at Jaxon and could easily see that their souls were kindred. This wasn't a synthetic human; this was a man, just like he was, both sharing the same needs, wants, and desires. Without hesitation, Larry quietly answered, "Of course I can."

Larry's words released Jaxon from his inhibitions. It was as if he was permitted to be himself, to open his heart, and to share with his friend how he truly felt about him.

Without any inhibition, Jaxon leaned forward and took Larry in his arms. He was desperate to feel Larry's lips against his. With his strong, muscular arms, Jaxon embraced Larry and drew him as close. He sweetly whispered, "We are safe, and I'll never let anything happen to you. I'm sorry you had to endure such a scare." Before kissing him for the first time, Jaxon again prepared to express his feelings, but Larry didn't want to hear any more words from him; he was too eager for another kiss. Lips, he believed, were better served pressed against another's mouth rather than forming sentences.

Jaxon briefly leaned back far enough to look at Larry's face. He looked deeply into his eyes and warmly stated, "Now that our mission is complete, we have no other duties to fulfill other than returning to earth. The next thirty days are strictly ours to do what we want... That said, I have a question. Have you ever made love in zero gravity? I've always wondered how it would be. I imagine it could be quite spectacular, and there's no one I'd rather experience it with than you."

Larry enthusiastically answered, "No. Can't say I've done it, but I will admit that it sounds like fun!"

Jaxon impishly reached across the console and clicked off the artificial gravity switch. The cabin lights switched to red, warning that the systems were off. The scarlet luminescence was seductive and sexy. The two men slowly became buoyant, each rising into the void of space.

"I think I'm going to like this experience," Larry chuckled. Jaxon eagerly agreed, "I hope so. I intend to make it something you never forget." As the two men's feet left the familiarity of the floor and they started freely floating through the air, they gradually began to undress each other amidst their kisses. As Jaxon reached to unclasp Larry's belt, the ship's intercom sounded, "Ares One. This is Houston. We detected a missed transmission from earlier today. Is everything okay? Is the mission proceeding as planned?"

After a brief moment to separate his lips from Jaxon's, Larry responded, "Yes, thank you, Houston. Everything's fine. The mission is on schedule." With a playful wink to Jaxon, he added, "Things are proceeding better than expected."

"Excellent. Thank you for the update," NASA responded before signing off. Jaxon again took Larry in his arms and whispered, "Now, where were we?" Larry answered in a mischievous tone, "I believe we were preparing to take off... our clothes."

The Gorgeous Gardener

T ucked away in the East Midlands of Britain lies Bakewell, a scenic village marked by narrow cobblestone streets teeming with townsfolk. Among them was Leo, a humble servant who navigated through these bustling lanes with skill and ease. The embodiment of youth and vigor, Leo was an enchanting figure known for his unwavering morals. Recently turned eighteen, his youthful vitality and zest for life were evident. Leo's broad shoulders and defined physique reflected his physical prowess and inner spirit. Every movement he made was purposeful and graceful, demonstrating a controlled authority.

As Leo navigated the town's charming thoroughfares, his purposeful footsteps resonated. He had just delivered a box of important invitations to the town crier and was now returning to his residence.

Though not truly a home, for it lacked warmth and family, his dwelling was actually a grand manor where he worked, slept, and lived. The impressive stone structure stood amidst the picturesque countryside. This stately dwelling belonged to a solitary stern nobleman named Lord Carlson.

Lord Carlson's mansion, imposing and austere, seemed to peer down upon the town with a stern presence. Its facade exuded rigidity and formality, leaving no room for warmth or joy. This had been Leo's residence since his childhood. He was an orphan taken in and raised by Lord Carlson's staff to serve in the household.

The cold, gray mansion was destined to be his home for the rest of his life, and the Lord, for lack of anyone else, was his surrogate father. Although Leo knew kindness from the other servants at the manor, he never felt love, as the staff did not seem to share Leo's empathy for Lord Carlson, finding him a hard, rigid man incapable of joy or emotion.

However, Leo frequently defended the Lord to the others, describing him as misunderstood, likely a man with a shattered past much like their own. He urged them to show compassion and understanding, even though the nobleman's harsh words and cold demeanor often cut through them.

***

On one particularly magnificent spring morning, Leo was summoned to the Lord's study. The master of the house cleared his throat with an icy crackle before commanding, "My duties as a lord in these regions require me to host an affair for the local aristocrats. I loathe these individuals and have nothing but disdain for my neighbors and surrounding nobility. Still, it is my duty to provide an exquisite affair in my manor and an evening they will remember. My roses are among my prized possessions, and my garden is my pride. I need you to meet with my horticulturist and prepare a magnificent bouquet of roses as the centerpiece of my table. Also, inform him that my private garden's gate is to be locked, and no one is to gain access during the affair. Anything less than a spectacular display from Julien will not be tolerated."

"Of course, Lord Carlson. It will be done immediately. I will meet with Julien now, explain your request, and inform him of your wish to keep the garden's gates locked during the gala," Leo replied. Without wasting a moment, Leo carried out the nobleman's instructions and made haste to the manor's back garden.

Lord Carlson's private orchard was nestled behind a topiary of shrubs shaped like various wild animals. Leo felt a thrill at the chance to visit the garden, which few had the privilege of stepping into, and to meet the gardener—referred to as "magnificently muscular and spectacularly handsome" by the women of the kitchen staff.

A strange sense of giddiness overwhelmed Leo as his pulse raced. Was he excited about the opportunity to visit a place that until now remained shrouded in secrecy, or about meeting another young man who intrigued the house staff?

***

A high stone wall surrounded the garden, the only access being a heavy wrought-iron gate. Though the gate was closed, the latch was unlocked. With Lord Carlson's permission, Leo entered the forbidden place, his heart quickening as he stepped through the gate.

In an instant, he was captivated by the blooming allure of the flowers, the sweet fragrance permeating the air, and the gentle rustle of leaves whispering Earth's secrets. Amidst this vibrant tapestry of nature, his senses were overwhelmed. He realized why the lord favored this place—its fragrant flowers and brilliantly blooming plants, all manicured to perfection, were the work of a master who had created a perfect sanctuary with divine assistance.

A deep, youthful voice called out from behind a chrysanthemum bush, "Hello. Can I help you?

Leo turned to meet his host and then gasped at the sight of the handsome young man. It was true what he had heard from the ladies in the manor. If anything, they had understated the gardener's appearance. His sun-kissed skin glowed with vitality, complementing his mesmerizing green eyes that sparkled with passion. His warm smile and trim, agile build, sculpted by dedication to the garden, embodied a natural charm that captivated all who crossed his path. Although his clothes were worn and dirt-smudged, they draped over his perfectly proportioned body like fine drapery.

Leo may not have addressed his sexual preference before, but now, one thing was abundantly clear - this was what he wanted. Julien was everything Leo had ever fantasized about in the deepest, most secret caverns of his mind, and now, his dream man stood before him.

"I'm... uh, Leo. Leo's my name." Leo did his best to sound articulate, but he was far from it.

The man continued, "I don't often get visitors here. I welcome the company and the sight of a fresh face. Especially one as fetching as yours." Julien pleasantly smiled as he reached out his hand in greeting. "I'm Julien. I was told you'd arrive and heard tales of your attractiveness, but I admit, you are even more dashing than I expected."

The two men shared a bashful chuckle, then Leo continued as if he hadn't received the compliment, "Then I suppose you know why I am here."

"Yes, I received a direct message from Lord Carlson earlier with instructions for the bouquet and a directive to keep guests out of the garden. I expect he sent you to ensure that I understood the urgency of his letter."

Leo nodded. "Yes, that could be it. It's curious that he sent me to convey something he had already put in writing, but no matter, I am glad to make the acquaintance of a man my age in this grand estate. "I don't know anyone other than the aged valets or the women from the kitchen staff."

"Yes, same here. I'm truly pleased to make your acquaintance. Perhaps, since the lord favors you as he does, he intended to send you here to treat you to a tour of his gardens? I'd happily show you our most prized possessions. Everything is in full bloom, and you'd be in for a treat. I take great pride in my work here. Nothing would please me more than to share it with you."

"I'D LOVE THAT!" burst from Leo's lips almost too enthusiastically. He quickly regained composure and politely stated in a reserved tone, "What a splendid idea."

Julien saw Leo's genuine appreciation for his garden and his reverence toward the living wonders surrounding them.

Instantly, a delicate yet profound connection sparked between the two young men. Within moments of spending time together, they knew that each other's company was all they desired.

In the days leading up to the grand gala, Leo would sneak out of his chambers each night to be at Julian's side in his garden. With Lord Carlson and the house staff deep asleep in the distant bedrooms of the mansion, Leo sought the sanctuary Julien's company provided.

Until meeting Julian, Leo hadn't considered his own sexuality. His tasks kept him occupied most of the day and night; he had precious little time to do anything but sleep.

Meeting Julian changed all that. His days were spent dreaming of the nights with Julian. Until this point, Leo believed that hard, dutiful work brought all the rewards he needed. But now, it was evident to him he was missing out on the very reason to be alive.

The very thought of Julian's lean, toned body, short, dark, shaggy hair, and welcoming, trusting eyes made Leo weak in the knees.

Strange that another fellow his age would make his heart race and his blood pump. What was this urge to kiss him? To feel his body pressed against his? To be as close to him as possible?

Three nights had passed since their initial encounter in this sacred garden. Each evening since then found them in the garden's most secluded nook, where they lay concealed by thorned rose bushes that served as vigilant guardians. As the sweet scent of blooming roses filled the air, they lay naked and entwined on a plush bed of moss. Their bodies warming each other against the chilly, damp night air. As close as they got to each other, it never seemed near enough. Not because of the cold but because of their desires. Julian's breath, his touch, his taste. Leo wanted it all, and each morsel made him crave more.

Unclothed and bathed in the soft, silvery glow of the full moon, their innocent, intertwined bodies made a solemn promise to each other. Their whispered words carried a profound promise, a shared dream of a day when they could rightfully call each other "husband."

***

The evening of the grand celebration had arrived, casting an enchanting glow upon the nobleman's mansion. Its opulent facade was bathed in golden candlelight, while the property sparkled with lanterns guiding guests towards the festivities. The fragrance of roses, Julien's masterpieces, mingled with the aroma of sumptuous delicacies served inside.

Amidst the bustling home now full of the local gentry, Leo stood at the central entrance. Dressed to the nines, he was the epitome of a diligent servant, ensuring every detail was perfect and orchestrating the seamless flow of the event.

As the gala raged inside Lord Carlson's grand ballroom, unbeknownst to anyone, an intoxicated guest known for his boisterous nature left the party and helped himself to a tour of the grand estate. After a self-guided tour of the cavernous and intricately adorned halls, he wandered through the animal-shaped bushes along the path toward the mansion's private garden.

Spotting Julien manicuring the topiaries, the nobleman waddled up to the gardener with a swagger and a stumble. "Young man, I would like to see the garden that produced this evening's flora.

Having seen the roses it has produced; I want to witness the garden in all its glory in person. Now, be quick with it and lead me to this magnificent arboretum."

Julien stood tall, dusting himself clean of the dirt and twigs that clung to his clothes. He was eager to present himself properly to the dignitary. "Yes, sir, the garden is indeed a sight to behold. It's the source of all my pride. I'd be thrilled to share it with you. However, as Lord Carlson's humble servant, I was instructed to keep the gates locked and politely decline any requests for entry. I apologize profusely for this inconvenience, but allowing admission is simply out of my control."

"HOGWASH!" The rotund aristocrat barked. "How DARE YOU refuse me?!" Once again, Julien apologized, trembling as the ruddy, obese man jabbed a finger into his chest. "I am a baron myself, and you are merely a servant. You are in no position to deny anything I request. Open the gates to the garden at once before I report your insolence to Lord Carlson! Refuse me again, and I assure you, you'll no longer have a place in this house, or any other manor in Britain!"

The man's intolerance and belligerence escalated, and despite his better judgment, fear of the man's wrath pushed Julien to unlock the imposing iron gates, granting him passage.

Julien watched in silent horror as the vulgar man carelessly trampled through the garden, destroying several of Julien's prized rose bushes and an array of shrubs adorned with crimson blooms.

Tears welled up in Julien's eyes as he cradled the broken stems. To him, these were not mere plants; they were living embodiments of his passion and dedication, each blossom a testament to his love for his craft.

His heartache was soon eclipsed by fear as he contemplated Lord Carlson's impending wrath upon discovering the state of the garden. The Lord's notorious temper, especially with regard to his roses, haunted his thoughts.

Would his master blame him for yielding to the terrible man's demands? Was he at fault for not maintaining his post as instructed?

Hidden in the garden, Julien agonized over the possibility of losing his position under Lord Carlson, and, worse, being separated from Leo.

The party ended, and Lord Carlson reveled in the success of the evening. Praise was lavished upon him by the other nobles in the area. Despite his claims of indifference to their criticism, the twinkle in his eye revealed that their acceptance meant the world to him.

Lord Carlson gathered his staff of eleven servants and lined them up. Before retiring for the evening, he wished to address his staff. Everyone was present but Julien. His absence wasn't a surprise to anyone; truthfully, no one thought to include him. This meeting was primarily for house staff. Julien was rarely, if ever, involved in the matters of the house.

Once assembled, the Lord briefly addressed the group. "This evening was quite spectacular. You all excelled at your jobs tonight. I am grateful for your efforts and talents. Goodnight."

As quickly as his remarks of gratitude were stated, so did the servants dissipate. Everyone was tired and eager for sleep. That is, everyone but Leo, who couldn't wait to slip away to reunite with Julien.

Leo found Julien in the garden; his usually vibrant spirit was replaced by fearful apprehension. Something was gravely wrong, and Leo was quick to take Julien into his arms to comfort him. "What has gotten you so upset? What happened tonight that I need to know about?"

Julien put on a brave face and took a deep breath. The sadness in his eyes told Leo the story, but it was the details he needed. Julien calmly recounted the terrible incident, "Tonight, as the grand celebration unfolded within the mansion's walls, an unthinkable calamity befell my beloved garden. An intoxicated guest, oblivious to the consequences of his actions, forced his way into the lord's sanctuary even after I forbade him to do so. I fear that Lord Carlson, in his disappointment and anger, may cast me aside, dismissing my years of service and devotion. The garden is my haven, my refuge, and the thought of losing both you and my roses breaks my heart."

Made aware of the gravity of the situation, Leo's heart now ached. He couldn't bear the thought of Julien suffering Lord Carlson's anger for a mistake he hadn't made. With a brave and stoic face, Leo proclaimed, "Tomorrow, I will make this okay; you needn't worry. Trust me, it will be fine. As of now, your only thoughts should be of this evening's success and the joy of being in my arms. Nothing else should concern you." A tender kiss between the two young men turned into a warm, comforting embrace as Julien nestled closely to Leo's chest, eager to hear the reassuring thump of his heartbeat echo through the tranquil silence.

***

The following day, Leo mustered the courage to request a private audience with Lord Carlson as the nobleman enjoyed his breakfast. This was an uncommon request, one that had never been made before, and it piqued the lord's curiosity. Intrigued, he granted Leo an audience in the grand library after his meal.

In the opulent library, beside a roaring fire, Lord Carlson settled into a plush, leather chair. He lit a pipe, leaning back to consider what his young servant wanted to discuss. As the woodsy aroma of the tobacco filled the room, Leo took a deep breath. His voice, steady yet infused with raw emotion, confessed his love for Julien, recounting their secret meetings under the pale moonlight in the garden, their stolen kisses concealed behind fragrant rose bushes, and their shared dreams of breaking free from societal constraints. He held nothing back, revealing every intimate detail, in the hope that Lord Carlson's sense of justice would appreciate the sincerity of his honesty.

***

Time stood still as Leo awaited Lord Carlson's response, his heart racing with anticipation. The suffocating weight of silence in the room grew with each passing moment, every second feeling like an eternity. When Lord Carlson finally rose from his seat, his features softened in the warm glow of the crackling fireplace. Leo braced himself for the worst, expecting a torrent of anger and disappointment to be unleashed upon him.

However, to his surprise, Lord Carlson walked toward the tall windows, his gaze fixated on the garden obscured by darkness. His eyes held a contemplative calmness, devoid of the rage Leo had feared. As he turned to face Leo, he steeled himself for the unknown.

"I have known you for many years, Leo," he began, his voice a delicate blend of softness and sternness. "Your unwavering loyalty and honesty have been pillars of strength in my life."

Lord Carlson then spoke of the transformation Julien had brought to the estate, Leo listened intently, his heart pounding. The nobleman's words were not laced with condemnation, but rather with deep understanding and appreciation for the love that had blossomed within the cherished grounds.

His voice carrying the weight of acceptance, he continued, "I may not comprehend the nature of your love, but I respect it. I respect both of you."

Leo felt as if a boulder had been lifted from his chest. His eyes welled up with tears of relief and gratitude. Lord Carlson's acceptance surpassed his wildest hopes. Overwhelmed by the nobleman's immense generosity, Leo managed to express his heartfelt thanks through choked words.

Lord Carlson raised his hand, signaling for silence. "Love knows no boundaries, Leo. Your connection with Julien has been evident in your unwavering dedication to this estate and each other. This is, and always will be, your home. Although you are both men, I consider you both my children. My home is your home, and the garden that Julien created is his. Please apologize to Julien for my guest's rudeness the other evening. I will address that issue. From now on, I will treat everyone in my employ as family, not as servants. I thank you for bringing this matter to me directly and honestly, and from this point forward, I promise to make this estate a worthy home for you all."

***

The days that followed saw a remarkable transformation within the manor. An unspoken understanding filled the halls, a newfound acceptance of Leo and Julien's love emanating among the staff and other household workers. Laughter echoed more freely, warmth infused the air, and their love became a beacon of joy in what was once a solemn abode.

With lighter hearts, Leo and Julien continued their service, liberated from the shackles of secrecy. Their love was no longer hidden in fleeting glances and stolen moments; it now shone freely under the sun's gaze. Their faces bore constant smiles, their hands were frequently intertwined, and they exchanged tender kisses openly. The garden reflected their joy, flourishing as vibrantly as their love.

The private midnight rendezvous between Leo and Julien continued in the garden, enveloped by the sweet fragrance of the prized roses. Each night at midnight bathed in the blue hue of the moonlight, their bodies drew close, their lips met, and their fingers traced the contours of each other's forms. One night, soon after the incident in the garden, Julien whispered to his beloved, "Never have I met a man with more character and bravery as you, I am truly lucky to call you my one true love."

Leo held Julien close, a smile lighting up his face, "My bravery is only matched by your passion, heart, and warmth. It is me who is the luckier of the two of us." His hand traced a path down Julien's lean, toned body, sparking a thrilling shiver of anticipation.

"Now, in this paradise that we've been fortunate enough to cultivate, on this perfect, warm summer's evening, I can think of no better time to make love to the man who is everything I've ever dreamt a man could be." Leo looked deeply into Julien's sweet, loving eyes as he softly caressed his face and replied, "Together, we will experience the gifts of intimacy for the first time. In my wildest fantasies, no evening, no place, or a person who has captured my heart could be more perfect."

And with that, their clothes fell away, piece by piece, each article dropped carelessly on the grass. Their disrobing was unhurried, each revealed skin awakening a new surge of desire, and soon they stood bare before each other. The cool night air caused goosebumps on their tender skin, a stark contrast to the fiery passion that ignited within them. Yes, Julien was known for his roses, but in this moment, it was his "tulips" Leo yearned for.

Acknowledgements

Writing is not a solitary endeavor. There are people along the way who contribute to every story.

I am grateful for their contributions, advice, encouragement, and support.

Silvia Calciano
Aunt Sue Urban
Matthew Solari
Julie A. Le
William Plyler
Susan McGrath Romito

More from
Steam Room Stories

We hope you enjoyed *Steam Room Confidential: Volume 5*.

But don't go away! There's plenty of fun to be had at SteamRoomStories.com.

Check out all our movies, books, podcast, and more!

Our Books

Buy all the *Steam Room Confidential* books and follow Cole as he collects more sexy stories from the bros in the steam room.

GAY SHORT STORIES

JC CALCIANO

STEAM ROOM CONFIDENTIAL

VOLUME 1

Steam Room Confidential: Volume 1

Threesome with the Ex
Tad believed that he and Lucas were the perfect couple. He couldn't believe it when his boyfriend Lucas wanted to have a threesome with another guy. Tad could never have expected that the other man Lucas invited into their bed was Tad's first love from high school!

Hottest Guy in the Bar
James lived in the trendy part of NYC's East Village. His favorite haunt was a bar down the street where a sexy man nicknamed "D.C." hung

out. D.C was an enigma, especially regarding where he got his nickname. Try as James did, he couldn't find much information on D.C. One incredible night, James discovered what D.C.'s nickname meant.

Bicycle Shorts

Randy just finished a day-long ride and was beat. A highway patrolman pulled him over as he headed home in his Jeep. "Where are you going, pretty boy?" The handsome, muscular cop asked. Randy couldn't help but flirt with this sexy officer. The hunky cop, at first, wasn't sure what to make of this fit young stud with a smart-ass attitude. Was this cocky young man asking for a lesson in dealing with the law or looking for a sexy rendezvous?

Prom Night Virgin

Joey and his best friend Bailey were the two best-looking seniors in high school. When prom came, there wasn't a girl in class who didn't want to be their date. The two boys chose the hottest girls to take to the dance. The two couples ended up having a blast at prom and finally headed out in their limo to a small motel room to get better acquainted for the night. Once alone, in the same room, it appeared that perhaps the two couples may have chosen the wrong partners.

The Sexy Stableman

Eighteen-year-old Charlie was desperate to lose his virginity to Dominque, a sexy French Au Pair who worked for his best friend's family. One summer, when she returned home, he decided to visit her and hopefully become a man. Upon his arrival in the small, quaint, remote European village she lived in, Charlie was eager to consummate the love affair he had dreamt about for the last five years. That was until he met Julien, the hunky stable man with whom he was now sharing a room. That he realized Dominque wasn't his only option in losing his virginity.

Ski Weekend

Aidan had just rushed the fraternity and was excited to meet all the brothers. When Studly alumni Karl entered the room, everyone gasped. "You're clearly my replacement around here," Karl confidently chuckled as he greeted the young freshman. "You do realize guys like us are only invited to rush this Fraternity as chick bait for the other brothers." Aidan knew he was right. His looks had opened a lot of doors for him at the university. Soon, his lean, muscular body and handsome face would afford him another invitation; to go skiing alone with Karl. The only question that remained was, would the two studs ever make it to the slopes, or would they spend the whole weekend in the chalet together?

My Boyfriend's Brother

Evan couldn't believe it when his boyfriend Durio broke up with him via text. Perhaps he was having trouble at home? Evan needed closure to this relationship. A quick ride to the country to Durio's parents' house to talk to him proved to be more than he bargained for. Not only did he meet Durio's ridiculously hot brother, but he also discovered that this gay sibling was more interested in him than Durio ever was. Perhaps Evan was with the wrong member of the family?

The Movie Star

Todd always dreamed of moving to California and working in the movie business. When he finally got his big break, he would have never dreamt it would be working for Sam Sterling, the biggest star in the world! Now Sam's assistant, Todd went everywhere Sam went. The two men became very close throughout their travels together. So close that it became difficult to tell where their business relationship ended, and their personal relationship began. Could it be that these two men's relationship was about to be more than just boss and employee?

Steam Room Confidential: Volume 2

A Farm Boy in Brooklyn
Bryce couldn't wait to start his career as an artist in Brooklyn. When he moved into a handsome Greek bouncer's New York brownstone, he had no idea that he'd lose his heart to him. How could Bryce deal with being in love with someone already in a relationship? Watching his roomie with his hunky boyfriend was too much to bear. He needed to decide what to do, and it seemed like leaving was his best option. However, it appeared that his roommate had other plans for him.

The Dream Man

Blake drove his convertible Jeep down to the beach and thought he spied his best friend nearby. Rather than it being his buddy, it turned out to be a stone-cold stud instead. Rather than the mix-up turning embarrassing, it somehow evolved into getting a few beers that night. Blake was shocked that the evening somehow turned into a racy rendezvous. Was the whole thing in his head? Did this hot, passionate night with his dream man really happen?

The Randy Repairman

John worked from home. When his computer failed to connect to the internet one morning, he called a repairman to fix it. The guy who showed up at the door was more than he could have expected or hoped for. This man was gorgeous! John knew that all he needed was the installation of a simple router, but he wasn't going to let this hunky repairman get away without making a few extra "house calls."

A Man with an Appealing View

Casey couldn't believe it when his best friend Deidra insisted he go out on a date with her landscape architect. He was done dating and certainly not interested in meeting some stranger. Casey knew it was easier to say yes, and just do what she said. When his date, Raphael, opened the door to his grand villa that overlooked the ocean, both the view and the hot hunk of a man before him took his breath away. Casey couldn't help but wonder if this stud was out of his league and if this date was a very bad idea.

A Charming Prince
Holt had just arrived in Los Angeles to attend law school. He decided to blow off some steam and visit Disneyland before his classes started. Holt knew Mickey Mouse and Goofy would be at the park to greet him, but he certainly didn't expect Prince Charming to ask him on a hot date and sweep him off his feet.

An Aussie Actor
James was happy being the only guy in acting class. He enjoyed being the stud all the girls desired. Suddenly that changed when a hunky Australian actor joined the group. James desperately wanted to know if the new guy was straight. Luckily, the instructor paired them up to perform a scene together in class. James decided to choose a hot, gay love scene to find out what was up with his new classmate.

The Hopeless Romantic
Lance loved romance. So much so that he decided to become a writer of gay love stories. When his books became popular, he was invited to participate in a popular writers convention. He was flattered to be invited to attend and had few expectations other than meeting a few fans. Lance certainly hadn't

planned on meeting a tall, handsome stranger who'd make the convention an occasion wilder and sexier than anything he could write in one of his romance novels.

A Very Happy Birthday

Riley wasn't looking forward to turning forty. He was still single and had never quite gotten over his first love, Wade. This year, an expected phone call from his friend from the past caught him by surprise. Of course, he declined the invitation to get together. But eventually, curiosity got the best of him. Does he still look as good as he did in college? Is he still with his wife? Riley decided to pass by his old friend's house just to see if he could get a glance at what had become of him. He could never have predicted what he would discover when he got to Wade's home.

Steam Room Confidential: Volume 3

Baywatch Bro
Dane assumed he'd never meet anyone working in a greasy spoon at the beach. Things changed when the head lifeguard, Lawrence, ordered delivery from his unassuming food stand. Dane soon looked forward to delivering lunch off to the sun-dipped Adonis every day. Who could have expected that the hunky lifeguard planned on Dane being on the menu one afternoon?

Mile High Club
Forrest had never been in an airplane before today. It was the first time he had ever flown, and he was

nervous. Forrest instantly felt at ease when he locked eyes with the hot, distinguished pilot who entered the plane. The flight took off without a hitch, and the long journey promised to be uneventful and relaxing. That was until the sexy Captain spotted Forrest seated by the cockpit and decided to show him just how friendly the skies can be.

The Muscular Mechanic

Dawson packed his bags and headed east on a quest to find inspiration for the great American novel he was writing. A quick bite at the local truck stop led to a chance meeting with a hunky mechanic named Leo. This random encounter with a rugged stud provided more than just an oil change for his car, but also just the erotic adventure he needed to complete the last chapter of his book.

A Stud for Supper

Everything was set for the perfect Thanksgiving celebration with the family. A last-minute call revealed that Taylor's sister invited her sexy co-worker to join them for dinner. His sister's guest was everything Taylor fantasized in a man. Now, Taylor couldn't be satisfied with the warm turkey on his plate when all he could think about was feasting on the hot stud sitting across from him at the table.

The Sexy Soap Star

It's been some time since Hudson's relationship ended. Finally, the time had come to get his own place and move out of his ex's apartment. This weekend he planned to go bargain shopping at local garage sales. Who could have predicted that the person having one of the sales was the sexiest soap opera star he'd ever laid eyes on? The moment Hudson laid eyes on him, he knew he wanted much more than a lamp and an end table!

Hunky Santa

Christmas was Dax's favorite holiday. Each year, he looked forward to leaving New York City and returning to Ohio to spend time with his family. Two days before Christmas, a freak snowstorm stranded him in Manhattan. It seemed that Dax wasn't going home anytime soon. Perhaps Santa has another gift in mind for him this year? Dax is about to learn that the best packages come with six-pack abs and bulging biceps.

School of Rock

Taylor always wanted to be a rock star, but his pragmatic parents insisted that he concentrate on his studies. On his 18th Birthday, Taylor secretly searched for a teacher to give him lessons. Nothing excited Taylor more than to learn how to play the guitar – but that was before he laid eyes on the sexy, long-haired rock-and-roller who would be his instructor. Now playing the electric guitar wasn't the only thing he wanted in his arms.

eCUPID 2.0

Jimmy started his day as usual–Single. When a mysterious app called *eCUPID* alerted him to the prospect of finding true love, he couldn't help but accept its terms and conditions. Suddenly his life was taken over by the gadget. Mysterious packages arrived, strange people appeared, and past relationships resurfaced... Was the app working in his best interest to find him love, or was this all some cruel joke being played on him?

Steam Room Confidential: Volume 4

Office Crush

Derek found the boss's new secretary too hot to handle. The sexy young hunk's tussled hair, bedroom eyes, and muscular body were precisely what he desired in a man. Derek worked in the executive mail room, and every day he excitedly waited for a package to arrive that required him to deliver it to the boss's office in hopes of catching a glimpse of this dream man. Derek knew his dirty daydreams about the studly assistant would one day get him into trouble. What he didn't know was that today would be that day.

Jock for Sale
When Brock, the hunky high-school quarterback, offered himself to be auctioned off at the local church fundraiser, every girl in the school bid for a date with him. Who would have guessed that it would be the soft-spoken, gay nerd would be the one to win the auction and a romantic dinner with the studly jock on Saturday night? When Saturday evening arrived, Brock showed up at Scottie's door to deliver his prize. Neither of the young men would have expected Saturday night's "dream date with the quarterback" would continue into a brunch on Sunday morning!

An Italian Affair
Jarrod's true love left him. He was heartbroken and wanted to lock himself away forever. A phone call from his aunt in Rome, Italy, forced him to travel to Europe to care for her. When a mysterious errand brought Jarrod within steps of the Trevi Fountain, the sights and smells of the ancient city instantly made him feel renewed. He couldn't help tossing in several coins and making a wish. Would this enchanted fountain provide the magic he desperately desired to heal his shattered heart?

Scout's Honor
Austin couldn't wait to leave the city and get into the great outdoors. He desperately desired to be alone so that he could enjoy the solitude of the

forest. Then loud music disrupted the silence of the woods. He was instantly agitated. *Where was this tune coming from?* he wondered. The answer to the mystery was a nearby campsite occupied by a hulking stud who was skinny dipping in the lake. Suddenly the song playing seemed quite pleasant, and his desire to be alone for the weekend changed into a yearning to snuggle by a campfire with this burly bro.

Golf Pro
Kaiden had just moved into the neighborhood and decided to visit the nearby nine-hole golf course and possibly take lessons to relax. When he entered the course's golf shop to inquire about classes and rent clubs, he didn't expect the man behind the counter to be as attractive as he was. The young pro was tall, tan, and tone–Kaiden was instantly smitten. Suddenly, golf was his new favorite sport, and he was quite eager to play with the pro who'd be teaching him.

A Haunted House
Mason Rogers was a scaredy-cat. He was so terrified of the old Karloff Estate on Ravenwood Road that his schoolmates nicknamed him "Scooby Doo." Nothing could make him walk down that creepy street. Well, maybe one thing could. Thad Thompson was the hottest hunk in town and lived next door to the old, abandoned manor. Every morning, Thad was shirtless in his driveway,

tinkering with his motorcycle. The sight of him working was just too yummy for Mason to pass up. Even though the old haunted house taunted him, he wondered, was this steamy stud worth mustering the courage to walk past the most haunted house in the town on Halloween Eve? Mason decided yes, it was.

Guy Friday

Today was Julian's opportunity to be the big boss at a Fortune 500 firm. He was convinced that he was prepared for his first day. His plans changed when his sexy, unabashedly flirtatious young "Guy Friday" showed up at his office door asking, "What can I get you this morning?" Now, Julian's first meeting of the day would take place in the executive washroom with his hot new male secretary.

World's Greatest Lover

It was Garrett's first day at Paramount Pictures. He was excited to work at the place that produced all his favorite movies. The famous old studio was brimming with historical artifacts. There was something unexpected in every corner, but none was more unforeseen than meeting a mysterious, sultry Italian actor named Rudolph. When Rudolph invited Garrett into his bungalow before shooting his love scene, Garrett quickly said yes. He couldn't help but hope that Rudolph wanted help preparing for his next shot.

Revenge of the Brobot: A Steam Room Story

*A softhearted stud and a rebel robot find
themselves on the run from a merciless Marine.*

Cutting-edge technology company Hot Bot-y Robotics
has created the perfect A.I. sexbot named ROB (Robot
with Organic Body). But when its creator learns that the
military wants to reprogram the robot into a state-of-
the-art killing machine, he sends ROB out into the
world to hide. As fortune would have it, ROB finds
sanctuary in a steam room of an old gym where he
catches the eye of a swoll stud named Chase. Can Chase
and his steam room bros save ROB's titanium tush from
a war-hungry General? Will the amorous android find
love and friendship with a sexy stud and his new ro-
bros?

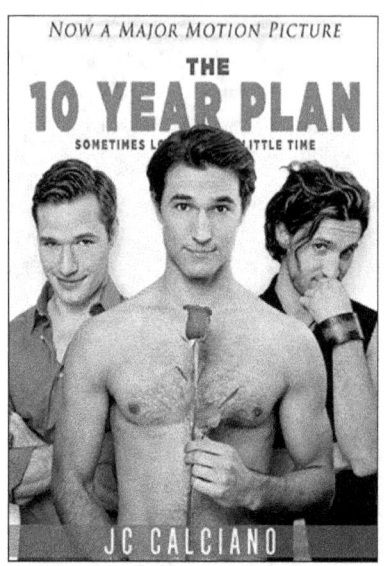

NOW A MAJOR MOTION PICTURE

THE 10 YEAR PLAN

SOMETIMES L... ...ITTLE TIME

JC CALCIANO

The 10 Year Plan

Best friends Myles and Brody are total opposites. Myles believes in true love and happily ever after; Brody believes in hot guys and lots of happy endings. But after Myles has a particularly bad date, they make a plan that, if they haven't found true love in 10 years, they'll become a couple. Ten years later…nothing has changed. Myles is still a hopeless romantic looking for Mr. Right, and Brody is still on the hunt for Mr. Right Now – both still alone. When they realize it's almost time to make good on the promise they made to each other a decade earlier, both friends scramble to do whatever it takes to avoid their fate: to be a couple! The search for each other's perfect partner is on! But maybe the man of their dreams is too close to see.

Bromantic Bliss – Adult Coloring Books

Ignite your passion with a splash of color!
Bromantic Bliss is an adult coloring book specially
designed for aficionados of male-male romance.
This coloring book features 35 tantalizing pages of
seductively drawn illustrations, showcasing a
captivating array of sexy men in love. Each
illustration is accompanied by playful, sultry, and
silly captions! Whether you're a fan of romance, a
coloring enthusiast, or simply looking for a fun,
relaxing escape, *Bromantic Bliss* promises an
unforgettable journey of artistic expression and
amorous delight.

Our Movies

Steam Room Stories: THE MOVIE

An Adventure of Brotastic Proportions.

Cosmetics magnate Sally Fay spends the last of her fortune to find the legendary Fountain of Youth and use the miracle water to save her sagging empire. With the help of a map, she discovers the ancient aquifer is located under a steam room gym in Encino, California. Sally will stop at nothing to possess the steam room and its magical waters. What she doesn't count on are the Steam Room Guys, who will do whatever it takes to thwart her evil plans and save their beloved steam room.

The 10 Year Plan

Sometimes Love Takes a Little Time.

Myles and Brody are two best friends who are total opposites. Myles is a hopeless romantic looking for Mr. Right. Brody is a sexy cop on the hunt for Mr. Right now. These two friends make a plan that they'll be together in a decade if they are both still single. Nearly ten years later and still alone, both friends will do whatever it takes to avoid becoming a couple.

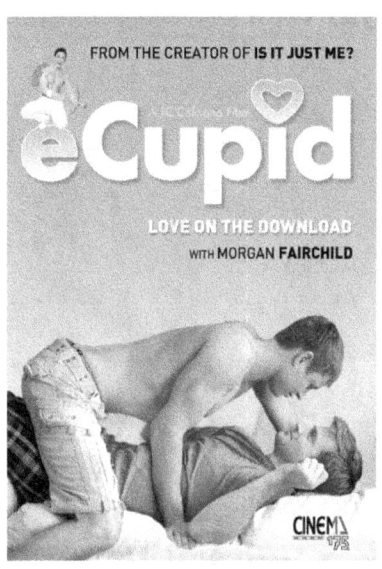

eCupid

Love On the Download.

This sparkling romantic comedy takes online dating to the extreme! Marshall is an over-worked ad exec suffering from a severe case of the seven-year itch with his loving boyfriend. As his 30th birthday nears, he is hell-bent on changing his life, and he comes across a mysterious dating app called eCupid. Turning his world upside down and overwhelming him with sexy, horned-up guys at every turn, Marshall gets much more than he bargained. Firing on all cylinders with sharp wit, hot cast, and even an extended cameo from Hollywood legend Morgan Fairchild, eCupid will win your heart.

Is It Just Me?

The Landmark Gay Romantic Comedy.

Laugh-out-loud funny and seductively sweet, Is It Just Me? is the landmark gay romantic comedy about one man's search for Mr. Right. Adorable Blaine can't seem to meet guys, let alone form a relationship. His beefy go-go boy roommate Cameron who has no shortage of willing partners, can't understand why he doesn't just pounce and enjoy some one-nighters. Instead, Blaine hides in chat rooms where he meets Zander, a shy, recently relocated Texan. But when the time comes to exchange photos, Blaine accidentally sends an image of his hunky roomie, and things go from romantically promising to downright confusing. Is It Just Me? is a bona fide feel-good winner full of witty charm and cute guys!

PODCASTS

Steamy Stories

Listen to all your favorite *Steam Room Confidential* stories on our popular podcast. *Steamy Stories* is where bromance becomes bromosexual!

A collection of sexy short stories written by JC Calciano and narrated by Ben Palacios & Casey Alcoser.

Available now on Apple Podcasts, Spotify, Google Play and more.

SteamyStoriesPodcast.com

About the Author

JC began writing books after a 30-year career as a filmmaker. His films include *Is It Just Me? eCUPID, The 10 Year Plan*, and *Steam Room Stories: The Movie.*

In 2010, he created the sketch comedy series for YouTube called *Steam Room Stories.* The show featured hunky, hot guys joking around in a steam room. It became an overnight sensation that continues to this day.

JC has also authored two novels: *Revenge of the Brobot* and a novelization of his film, *The 10 Year Plan.*

Steam Room Confidential is a collection of his short stories from the popular podcast *Steamy Stories.*

JC enjoys writing and reading m/m romance and camp comedy. His signature sense of humor is undeniably present in all his works.

Join the Fun!

VISIT
Go to SteamRoomStories.com to watch the movies, see the series, and read the books.

SUBSCRIBE
Sign up for JC Calciano's Cinema175 Newsletter for news and giveaways at JCCalciano.com.

FOLLOW
JCCalciano.com
SteamRoomStories.com
SteamyStoriesPodcast.com
Cinema175.com